Guns on the Wahoo

Fargo Reilly arrives in the town of Verdad de Soleil just as the local rancher, Lucas Carter, looks set to tighten his stranglehold.

Reilly seems like a harmless drifter, but after demonstrating his skill with a Colt on Carter's son and thrashing the hulking ranch foreman, things begin to change. In truth, Reilly is a federal marshal.

Events take a tangled course and Reilly must use some double dealing and chicanery. Only then can he silence Carter and the *Guns on the Wahoo*.

Guns on the Wahoo

GEORGE J. PRESCOTT

A Black Horse Western

ROBERT HALE · LONDON

© George J. Prescott 2006
First published in Great Britain 2006

ISBN-10: 0-7090-7959-1
ISBN-13: 978-0-7090-7959-0

Robert Hale Limited
Clerkenwell House
Clerkenwell Green
London EC1R 0HT

Typeset by Derek Doyle & Associates, Shaw Heath.
Printed and bound in Great Britain by
Antony Rowe Limited, Wiltshire.

CHAPTER ONE

The combined editorial office and print room of the *Verdad Tribune* was a mess. True, the giant Gutenberg rolling press stood four square and undamaged on its ugly German framework, but every other movable item, type, ink, paper, even the editor's battered old roll-top desk had been wantonly spilled across the floor.

In the midst of the wreckage lay Eustace Grafton, the *Tribune* owner, editor and sole reporter. The old man was bleeding from a long deep cut on his forehead, inflicted by the foresight of a Colt revolver in the hands of one of his attackers, and his grandaughter, Millie, was trying to staunch the copious flow of blood that persisted in making its sluggish way down his forehead.

'Those damn cowards!' the girl stormed, 'If I was a man, Grandpa . . .'

'You'd be dead now,' the old man interrupted softly. 'That scum beat up old men who get in their way, but they kill young ones. Speakin' of which, where's Arnie?'

As if in answer to the old man's question, the street door slammed back on its hinges admitting a figure covered in a liberal dousing of tar to which was fixed the filthy contents of an old feather pillow case. A voice, barely recognizable as Arnie Pauling, Grafton's typesetter, issued from this apparition.

'Mistah Grafton,' it quavered, 'them Diablos done this to me, they said 'cause I work fer you. So I'm quitting afore they do the rest of what they said they'd do! You can bring any money you figure I'm owed to the hotel.'

Pauling had not been gone many minutes, when Grafton gently disengaged his granddaughter's soothing fingers and slowly forced himself to his knees.

Painfully, the old man eased himself upright and stiffly, favouring his left side, managed to tip up the old desk and the even older swivel chair that belonged to it. Gratefully, he sank into the worn old leather and leaned back, eyes closed.

'Millie, my love,' he began, after the first dizziness had passed and the pain in his chest had begun to ease down to manageable proportions, 'I think it's time we thought about you goin' back to that fancy Eastern college o' yours.'

Smiling tolerantly, the girl leaned over the old man and planted a kiss on his aching forehead.

'No,' she said simply, 'and I'm not going to talk about it either!'

For a moment, the old man examined her in the flaring light of the lamp she was lighting, then he said simply:

'An' I thought your Grandma was the stubbornest female I ever run across!'

'I'm not stubborn, Grandpa,' the girl returned, 'just know my own mind is all. Besides, the cowards wouldn't dare touch me. They know Uncle Bud'd hunt down and hang every Diablo on the range if they tried.'

Carefully, the old man shook his head.

'You don't know your godfather if'n you think that. I couldn't see him wastin' either time or rope if he had a six-gun handy. Not if they'd hurt you.'

Bleakly, he examined the contents of the wrecked office and as he looked the girl was amazed to see the beginnings of a smile break across his face. Before she could speak the old man slapped his thigh and, after cursing fiercely at the pain this action caused his already aching head, exclaimed:

'Ain't I a goddam fool, though! Here I am worrying about this mess and not thinking clear enough to see what it means, girl.'

For a moment, Millie looked puzzled, then she said, 'All right, Grandpa, I admit I'm dumb but what does it mean?'

But Grafton was already straightening the type box before collecting a handful of the scattered letters and beginning to distribute them into the labelled boxes. Millie repeated her question and this time the old man looked up.

'It means that whatever I been sayin' about Carter in the *Tribune* has got him scared. Which means it's true about the land deals and all the other stuff. He wants that land bad, although what use he's got for

7

burned over prairie is more than I could tell you.' He paused for a moment, lost in thought.

Millie took advantage of the lull to say, 'Grandpa, it was the Diablos done this and tarred and feathered Arnie because of what you've been writing about them. You got no proof Carter had anything to do with it or them. And what about that letter you wrote to the Governor. He's supposed to be your friend, why isn't he helping?'

'Goddam it!' Grafton exploded, characteristically vehement, 'I knew Joe Clements when we was both workin' on the *Frisco Star*. He wouldn't have let an *amigo* down then an' bein' governor won't ha' changed him that much. I'm bettin' high we'll hear from him soon!'

'And even if I can't prove it,' he went on more calmly, 'I know them Diablo skunks work for Carter. Everything they've done has helped that bas— fella some way.'

'Well, I just hope that governor friend of yours sends some help soon, Grandpa,' the girl said doubtfully. 'It can't come too quick for me!'

'Meantime,' she went on, pulling on Pauling's grubby, ink-stained apron as she spoke, 'looks to me like you need a new typesetter.' She paused and finished thoughtfully. 'Perhaps you should put a card in the window.'

At that moment, in a dusty little town in Arizona, the Wells Fargo agent was delivering a letter, by the simple expedient of passing it across his counter. Its recipient would have attracted notice nowhere. Just a lean cowboy approaching middle age, he'd been mild, almost diffident in his request for mail and even the two worn-butted Colts in the fast-draw belt hadn't impressed the clerk enough to remember the name he'd given. He watched without interest as the cowboy rapidly scanned the letter, then stuffed the two close-written sheets in the pocket of his denim jacket. The agent hadn't even been concerned enough to examine the grubby envelope that had gone with the letter, either. If he had he would have seen the return address given as 'Office of the Territorial Governor'.

Once back in the town's only livery stable, where his already saddled pony awaited him, the cowboy hitched himself on to the edge of the old, tooth–gnawed water trough and began to construct and smoke a cigarette, whilst apparently deep in thought.

Eventually, he seemed to make up his mind and, rising slowly to his feet, removed the Colts from their holsters, wrapping each carefully in cloth and placing them together in an oilskin bag that went into one of the capacious saddle-bags hanging from the saddle of his stocky paint mustang. The fast–draw belt followed but not before he had drawn a second belt from the saddle-bags, loaded the pistol it contained and fitted it snugly around his lean waist. The blue eyes, which had never ceased to scan that part of the street and its surroundings visible through the open door of the building, were hard as, his disguise complete, he swung aboard the pony, but his voice was soft as he spoke, half to himself.

'Guess we'll have to trust to luck that nobody notices the rifle. Got to have some kinda equalizer handy.' His mount snorted in answer and the man grinned, his eyes and face softening.

'You figure our luck's stretched kinda thin already, do you?' He conceded, 'Well you might be right at that, son, you might just be right at that.'

Gently, the cowboy turned his mount out of the livery stable and up the dusty street, without apparently noticing the two Mexicans who ran for their mounts and quietly followed him.

Pedro, the leader of the pair, was explaining the situation carefully to his friend as they surveyed the gringo's camping ground later that evening, long after darkness had fallen with the swiftness characteristic of the South-West.

'You see, Carlito,' he finished, 'the gringo, he is verra stupid. He leaves the nice leetle pony far away from his hand, just where a man might happen to find it and ride it away. And Señor Jordan, he will pay well for killing this man who make the law hang his son.'

'I don' thin' he is so stupid, *amigo*,' Carlito offered dubiously. 'A man in his line of work, he don' stay alive long if he is careless as this one makes out.'

'Pah,' Pedro dismissed his friend's doubts with a single derogatory expletive. 'Go down and get the nice leetle pony, Carlito,' he ordered imperiously. 'I will take care of the gringo.'

This taking care of proved slightly more difficult than Pedro had envisaged, because as he made his way carefully past the gringo's fire to where the blanket-wrapped figure apparently slumbered, the shrill scream of a fighting mad mustang suddenly split the air. Showing no hesitation, Pedro covered the distance between himself and the sleeping gringo and slammed three slugs into the blanket-wrapped shape before the figure could move.

'Now what did you have to do that for?' a diffident voice enquired from behind the Mexican. 'That blanket ain't no use at all now.'

Knowing himself caught, Pedro didn't hesitate. He twisted, snapping up his pistol as he did so, only to be caught in the chest by the first of the cowboy's bullets, fired from the cover of a low saguaro cactus that he'd switched to as soon as darkness covered his movements. A second shot instantly followed the first, driving into the Mexican's head, although the cowboy's first had done all that was necessary.

Several minutes passed, then the cowboy's head appeared from behind the sheltering cactus. Carefully, he moved through the meagre brush until he could squat silently, within clear sight of his victim.

Only when the sun had risen, giving a clear view of the previous evening's carnage, did the man rise from his squatting position in the brush and move noiselessly to attend to his now silent pony and the red stamped thing which had once been Pedro's timid *amigo*, Carlito.

Just over a week later, that same unassuming cowboy eased the reins of his tired pony on the last rise before the main street of the little New Mexican town

11

of Verdad de Soleil. Cautiously, because caution was as much a part of his make-up as the blue of his eyes, he scanned the street and the warped clapboard and adobe buildings that lined it.

'That must be the *Tribune*'s office down there,' he decided, adding whimsically, 'and the livery stable right next door, which I'm guessin'll be more in your line, ol' timer.

As if in reply, the powerful little paint nickered softly and, encouraged by the gentle urging of the man's spurless heel, ambled down the slope towards the building in question. A tickle on the reins brought the pony to a halt and the man swung down, carelessly dropping the reins in the street as he did so.

Without a glance at his mount, he crossed the well-made wooden sidewalk and stood for a moment perusing the neatly lettered sign stuck squarely in the middle of the newly repaired window.

Apparently satisfied, he turned and knocked softly at the glass-fronted door of the *Tribune*'s main and only office. Grafton looked up from his desk. His look was a question and the cowboy grinned sheepishly, dragging off his wide-brimmed sombrero before jerking a thumb at the neatly lettered board in the window.

'About that job . . .' he began.

'And I figure a spell o' town livin' and inside work'd mebbe suit me right well, an' ol' Pecos won't complain none,' the cowboy finished, gesturing at the powerful little pony who waited in the street, ground-hitched and patient, for the return of his master.

Thoughtfully, Grafton studied the man who had offered his services. A first glance took in the faded range clothes and the battered, dusty Stetson, the air of calm confidence about the man. This was one who avoided trouble, who took most of what happened in his stride. And the old percussion Remington, converted for centre fire cartridges, was no gunman's weapon.

But there was something . . . perhaps just the way the old pistol hung, maybe, and the fact that his hands rarely strayed far from his belt, as though something was usually worn there that both hands had a use for,

Still, a man plainly not looking for trouble, perhaps because trouble had a way of finding him. Cold blue eyes returned his scrutiny and, abruptly making up his mind, Grafton thrust out a hand.

'Glad to have you with us, son.' He paused, considering, then went on, 'Since you're stickin' around, what'll we call you?'

'You can call me what you like, as long as you don' call me late fer meals,' the stranger answered with a grin, 'but most folks call me . . . Reilly. Fargo Reilly.'

CHAPTER TWO

Later that evening, after supper, Grafton got down to cases.

'This job ain't gonna be no cinch for you,' he began bluntly. 'Last fella got tarred and feathered before them Diablo skunks run him out.'

'He ain't me,' Reilly stated flatly. 'Feathers make me sneeze,' he went on whimsically, 'so I'm figgerin' to stay well away from them.'

'You may not get the choice,' came the waspish reply. 'About five years ago,' Grafton went on, 'fella name of Lucas Carter sashayed into town, pockets full of money, and began buying up everything in sight.'

'Just what sort of "everything"?' Reilly interrupted.

'That was the funny part.' Grafton admitted. 'There didn't seem to be no plan to it that you could put your finger on. He bought Austin Mainridge's store and the saloon, but never bothered about anything else in town. He ain't got a house here even, nothing like that.'

'What else?' Reilly prompted gently.

'Oh, he picked up the title to a lot of range along both sides of the Wahoo,' Grafton offered pensively.

'So, whatever his plan is,' Reilly said, 'he needs a lot of water. He must've had to pay plenty for them pieces,' the cowboy went on thoughtfully.

'Got 'em dirt cheap,' Grafton snapped, 'on account of the owners being driven off by a gang o' coyotes callin' theirselves the Diablos.'

Conversation lapsed, both men deep in thought, and more for something to say than because she was interested, Millie asked, 'Fargo's an unusual name, Mr Reilly. Is it a family name?'

'Ain't got no family to speak of, ma'am,' Reilly admitted, with a dry smile. 'My ma was found in the back of a Wells Fargo stagecoach, shot full o' Comanche arrows. She'd held me in front of her the whole time, shieldin' me, so I weren't hurt a bit. Mr Reilly, that was the station agent, said she died about an hour after they got her out of the coach. Never had no papers, not even a weddin' ring, so Mr Reilly took me in.'

For a moment, Reilly paused and the cold blue eyes softened.

'Ol' Frank Reilly never got around to givin' me a first name but folks took to callin' me the "Wells Fargo" kid. That got shortened to Fargo and it stuck,' he finished with a shrug.

'And you never found any of your folks?' Millie asked sympathetically, while snatching a swift glance at the clock and ignoring her grandfather's warning scowl.

'Nope,' Reilly answered with a smile. 'Ol' Frank

died in the last year o' the war and there was nothin' keepin' me so I lit out. Been a rollin' stone ever since.'

'Must be hard, having no family, not knowing where your roots are,' the girl went on artlessly, as she rose and began to gather up the dishes, only to drop one with a clatter as the sound of a whip-poor-will, calling twice, echoed from the night-time darkness.

'I guess what you ain't never had, you can't much miss.' Reilly shrugged, but there was a chilly finality in his tone which discouraged further questions, so with another glance at the clock, Millie carried her laden supper tray into the kitchen.

'She's only a kid,' Grafton excused, as the door banged behind his granddaughter, 'she didn't mean nothin'.'

'Never thought she did,' Reilly responded mildly. 'Only way you learn anything, askin' questions. Speakin' o' which,' he went on, 'was there anythin' else Carter bought or tried to buy in town that might give a pointer to what he's up to?'

'Well, there was one thing he wanted,' Grafton began, 'but the old coot of an owner was too stubborn to sell—'

But whatever else he was about to say was interrupted by a piercing whinny from the region of Grafton's tiny horse-corral.

'Miz Millie likely to have gone outside?' Reilly snapped, rising in one swift movement to turn down the lamp and move catlike to the outside door.

'N-no . . . well . . . mebbe,' Grafton prevaricated.

'Lock the door and stay inside,' Reilly ordered quietly, reaching for his gun-belt.

'Sure . . .' Grafton began, but he was talking to himself.

Warm darkness enfolded Reilly as he slipped noiselessly across the sun-dried timbers of the porch to where he could peer round the corner of the building nearest the corral. After that one shrill warning, Pecos had made no further sound but that didn't fool Reilly.

The corral lay bathed in moonlight and Pecos was moving restlessly at the farthest end, glaring at something which lay hidden in the darkness. Patient as an Indian, Reilly slipped off the porch and, hugging the shadows of the wall, made his way silently to the back of the house.

About to ease himself round the corner, he jerked back at the sound of a man's voice emanating from somewhere near the rear porch.

'But, *querida*,' the voice said, 'how can your grandfather make the problem? I love you and you love me and we jus' want to be married. How can he say no? Mebbe it is that you are not sure?' the man finished accusingly.

'Oh, Luis, how can you say that?' Millie Grafton began, but Reilly didn't stay to listen. Whatever had spooked Pecos, it wasn't the two lovers on the porch, nor the boy's horse, a dainty palamino, which was tethered to a veranda post. And it was still there, because Pecos hadn't moved from the end of the corral.

Swiftly, Reilly moved back to the front of the building before angling off in a wide circle, which brought him, minutes later, to the shelter of a meagre sagebrush, from where he could see both the corral and the back of the house.

Grafton's house lay on the outskirts of Verdad and was surrounded by a number of adobe and clapboard structures, now abandonded by their owners. Glaring into the darkness, Reilly tried to envisage the direction of Pecos's fixed stare and moments later, from a corner of one of the tumbledown dwellings, a red eye winked at him.

Reilly grinned into the darkness. Anyone stupid enough to smoke while they were watching someone in that inky blackness wouldn't be hard to locate and should be even easier to deal with.

Silently, he rose to his elbows and crawled swiftly towards the watcher. Angling so as to keep the sagebrush screen between him and his quarry, Reilly reached a point about a hundred yards behind the figure, who, oblivious to his presence, continued to smoke and watch the couple on Grafton's porch.

Hidden by a corner of crumbling adobe, Reilly was easing to his feet while slipping the old Remington from its holster, when a dry, whirring rattle sounded from a crevice next to his ear and a writhing shape shot past his face. Shaken out of his habitual composure, Reilly jerked back, losing his balance and his weapon at the same time, before measuring his length in the dust.

Shaken, but unhurt, he lunged to his feet to find the rattler and the man he had been watching both vanished and only the sound of swiftly running feet mocking him from the darkness.

Using a piece of sun-dried sagebrush, Reilly located his pistol and was carefully blowing the dust off the weapon as he walked through the back door of Grafton's house and into the kitchen.

Millie was there, making a pretence of doing the dishes. She jerked her head up as Reilly slipped through the door.

'Oh,' she gasped, 'I thought . . .'

'He'd come back for something,' Reilly finished drily. 'You might tell your young fella,' the cowboy went on with a smile, 'that whip-poor-wills don't usually come this close to town.

'Best thing you could do if you want to signal around here is bark like a hound dog,' he went on, matter-of-factly, 'but you don't never want to use bird calls, especially after dark.'

'Really, Mr Reilly,' the girl bridled angrily, 'and do you include snooping amongst your other areas of expertise?'

'No ma'am,' Reilly answered mildly, 'but someone else sure does. I found a fella watchin' the pair o' you on the porch, which was the only reason I stayed out there. And come to think of it,' he finished, 'why don't the pair of you do your sparkin' in the front parlour, like normal folks?'

For a moment, the girl's eyes flashed fire and Reilly thought perhaps he had gone too far. Then her mouth twisted and she slumped into a kitchen chair, her face a picture of misery.

'You're right, Mr Reilly,' she said tiredly, 'only, you see, Luis is a Mexican and it might not look right to the good people of this town for a Mexican boy to come courting a white girl ... and as for Grandfather ... she sighed, 'I can't imagine what he'd say!'

'This young fella, what is he, cowhand, sheep herder, somethin' like that?' Reilly asked mildly.

'I should just think not,' Millie flared immediately. 'His father is Don Raoul Sanchez and he was the biggest landowner in these parts before Carter butted in. They own Black Mountain where it dips down into the valley of the Wahoo, just up beyond the painted rocks and Luis says one day, if the railroad ever comes and they can get enough water, it'll pretty near feed the whole state!' she paused, blushing as Reilly's grin broadened, before finishing in pretty confusion.

'Well, he did! And he'll do it, too. One day.'

'Sure,' Reilly said gently, with a smile that contained more in it of memory than perhaps even he would have cared to admit, 'but for now, who do you think might have been watchin' the pair o' you?'

'I've no idea,' the girl admitted. 'Some of the boys around town are very jealous of Luis, but we've always been very careful not to give anyone reason to make trouble, although that hasn't stopped some of Carter's men. Why?' she demanded abruptly, unaccountably frightened by Reilly's thoughtful look.

'Oh, it's probably just me getting scared o' nothing,' Reilly lied easily. 'Although,' he admitted to himself, as he rose and moved towards the door of the dining-room where Grafton waited impatiently, 'I sure would like to know just who that *hombre* was watching tonight.'

20

'By the way,' he finished, pausing with his hand on the knob of the door, 'was I you, I'd give your grandpa a chance to get to know that young fella. He may just surprise you.' He was gone before she could think of a suitable retort.

'Oh, it weren't nothing after all,' Reilly explained in answer to Grafton's barrage of questions, as he poured a cup of coffee he didn't want from the simmering pot on the fire.

'Ol' Pecos is gettin' old and a mite nervous. Sometimes he thinks he sees things that ain't there. Like most o' us cow wranglers. I figure the ol' fella's been kicked in the head one too many times. You was tellin' me about Carter and his buyin' spree,' he prompted rapidly, before the older man had a chance to reply.

'Like I said, there was one other place Carter wanted to buy,' Grafton went on pensively, as Reilly dropped back into his seat, 'but that ain't ever gonna be for sale 'til the owner's in the ground! I . . . Owner told him so, too!'

'Oh, Reilly answered, 'and what might that be?' although Grafton's slip had given the cowboy all the information he needed.

'Why, the *Tribune*, o' course!' the old man snapped testily. 'So now you can figger just about what sort of hornets' nest you've landed yourself in!'

Reilly sat back, smiling slightly. It was nice when the pieces started to fit so neatly this early in the game.

CHAPTER THREE

Before returning to the back room of the cantina where he was staying, Reilly unrolled the battered tarpaulin from his bed roll and used it to cover the spot where the man he had found watching Grafton's house had lain.

He was out of his blankets with the dawn the next morning, as usual, and without waiting for breakfast, made his way to the crumbling adobe which faced his new employer's back door, where his tarp lay anchored against the dawn wind.

Being careful not to disturb the ground beneath, Reilly eased back the cover and examined the marks the man had left behind.

He'd been on the small side, this watcher in the dark, with the pointed-toe boots and bowlegged walk of a cowhand. A white man, too, or the dozen discarded cigarette butts, rolled in store-bought paper and containing tobacco with the pungent and unmistakable odour of Bull Durham, lied. Not much else to tell, Reilly admitted, he'd taken off fast when he'd heard Reilly behind him, which made him either smart or scared. Looking at the depth of his toe prints as he sped away, Reilly was willing to bet on the former.

Grafton found his new employee waiting on the porch when he came to open the newspaper office and the old man glanced with mild disapproval at the snoozing figure, booted feet wedged on the hitching rail, Reilly's freshly shaved face covered by the battered Stetson.

Grafton backed silently away and picking up a handful of gravel from the roadway, tossed a couple of pieces at the sleeping cowboy until Reilly stirred and rubbed a long-fingered hand across his mouth. More than one Westerner had died with a surprised look on his face because he had been careless about waking his side partner.

Carefully, Reilly picked a piece of the offending gravel from his shirt and examined it judiciously before dropping it back in the roadway. He rose languidly, but there was no sleep in his voice as he said, 'I didn't know you was ever a drover, Mr Grafton.'

'Done a heap o' things, young man,' the old editor admitted, 'and I learned early that, out here, it don't pay to be careless wakin' a man who carries a gun, even an old misfire like that,' he finished, pointing disparagingly at Reilly's side arm.

'She's good enough for me,' the cowboy shrugged, 'but I'm guessin' I won't need her in this line o' business.'

'Nope,' Grafton admitted, 'but one thing you will need is a good shirt and a pair of town pants. Cowhands don't suit a newspaper office.' The old

23

man finished with a deprecating shrug.

'Why sure,' Reilly admitted sheepishly. 'I should ha' thought o' that my own self. I'll just go get me some store-bought duds and be right back.'

'Tell Eli to put it on my bill, if'n you need to. . . .' Grafton began.

'Naw, I ain't broke,' Reilly admitted easily. 'You'd sure be surprised how many people between here and the bend o' the Canadian, don't know the first thing about poker,' he grinned, by way of explanation.

The store was large and well stocked, something of a surprise in a little out of the way town like Verdad de Soleil. Having completed his purchases, Reilly said as much to Eli Finch, the counter clerk, who shook his head at such naïvety.

'There's a couple of Mex cow-trails cross the border, just a little bit east of here,' the man explained, 'and even if we didn't get no trade from them, why, Mr Carter's operation'd sure take up all my time.'

'Big outfit, huh?' Reilly asked conversationally, as he perched himself comfortably on a handy flour barrel and began to construct the inevitable cigarette.

'You better believe it, mister,' the counter hand said enthusiastically. 'Big and gettin' bigger all the time! They're always looking for good men, too, the way I hear it,' he finished meaningly.

'Oh, I already got me a job,' Reilly assured him artlessly, without apparently noticing the almost silent arrival of two newcomers.

Both were clearly cowhands and the first man, shorter and much younger than his companion, led the way to the back of the store with a cocky assurance that might have been responsible for the look of settled contempt with which his companion regarded him. Halting within earshot of the pair at the counter, the younger man pulled out a sack of Bull Durham tobacco and began to roll a smoke.

'You do much business with the Sanchez outfit?' Reilly went on when his companion showed no sign of moving towards his new customers.

Clearly this was the wrong question, because the smile on the clerk's face froze and, after a nervous glance in the direction of the two cowhands, he said nervously, 'I work for the Carter outfit, mister, and I just sell to who I'm told to!'

'So, what you mean is, Mr Carter won't let you sell to the Sanchez ranch?' Reilly probed mercilessly.

'Look, mister . . .' the clerk began but he was saved from further committing himself by a youthful voice which snapped at them.

'And just why in hell would you be poking into my father's business, *hombre*?'

Reilly turned to see the younger of the pair of cowhands strutting towards him, while his companion followed with a look of long-suffering despair on his face. The younger man was dressed in the height of store-bought cowhand fashion, all frills and buckskin, while round his waist was buckled a fast-draw gun-belt supporting a pair of pearl-handled, silver-mounted Colts. Reilly sighed mentally. Kids acting tough always brought out the worst in him.

'Name's Reilly, Fargo Reilly.' Reilly answered carefully, 'I just started workin' on Mr Grafton's newspaper and figured I'd just get to know how the land lay.'

'How the land lay?' the youngster sneered, 'I'll tell you how the land lays, you goddam two-bit drifter. My father owns everything in this town worth ownin' and he's about due to tie up the rest of the valley right soon. Then Grafton an' all that other scum'll be dancin' to our tune.'

'Nice to be certain of so much,' Reilly answered gently, picking up his packages and walking towards the door. 'I guess it comes o' being young and . . . real stupid.'

'Why, you goddam worthless son of a bitch,' the younger Carter bellowed and, ignoring his companion's warning shout, the youngster broke into a run that took him through the street door just as Reilly reached the first step of the porch.

Only Reilly didn't take the step. As Carter reached out to grab him, Reilly took hold of a pole used to support the veranda roof and swung smoothly away from his attacker, while Carter stumbled across the top step to land bruised and winded, face down in the street.

Arriving a couple of seconds later, Carter's companion found Reilly leaning on the post he'd used to such good effect, while Carter alternately moaned and scrabbled in the dust, desperately trying to pull air into his abused lungs.

'Is he always this stupid?' Reilly asked mildly as the cowhand, who was tall and lean as a Brazos steer, settled himself comfortably on the other side of the post while he perused the ineffectual efforts of what was clearly his employer's son.

'Rafe's got about as much sense as a cow turd,' came the surprising retort. 'He's as mean as his daddy but he ain't got the brains God gave an ant. Name's Travis, knowed by most folks as Long Travis, on account of I ain't got my growth yet,' the cowboy went on, extending a hand like a paddle. 'And I'm here to say you sure handled that li'l bastard neat.'

'Is his daddy gonna take kindly to you an' me jawin' friendly like this?' Reilly asked, as Carter began to struggle to his feet.

'Ain't sure,' Travis admitted, 'but it's too hot to argue.'

'I'm agreein' with you,' Reilly began as he stepped down into the street, neatly evading Rafe Carter's first maddened rush and planting a boot square in the seat of the boy's fancy buckskin pants as he lunged past. With almost sight-defying swiftness, Reilly plucked one of Carter's pistols from his belt and flicked open the loading gate as the boy once again measured his length in the dust.

'Tut, tut,' Reilly said critically, turning towards his erstwhile attacker, 'now this is a nice pistol, why don't you get someone to show you how to keep it clean? It'd sure work a whole lot better.'

Almost incoherent with rage, Carter staggered to his feet. He backed a few paces from Reilly and his right hand came up to hover over his remaining pistol.

'You know so much about guns,' the youngster sneered, 'why don't you show me how to use one?'

'Sure,' Reilly answered with a shrug, then his left hand was blurring the hammer of the borrowed Colt.

His first shot tore the remaining pistol from Carter's belt, his second sliced the boy's shoulder, inflicting a graze and turning Carter half round while the remaining bullets tore the top three buttons from Carter's fancy shirt front.

'Like I said,' Reilly offered, matter-of-factly, 'a nice weapon.' Then, seeing the look of stunned surprise on Carter's face, he went on. 'You better take him home, Long, afore he wets hisself.'

'Sure,' the cowboy agreed, before adding carefully. 'Do me a favour, will you, friend? If I ever look like I'm gonna be stupid enough to pull a gun on you, don't let me, please.'

'Oh I ain't that good,' Reilly answered disparagingly. ' 'Sides, parlour tricks is one thing, a real gunfight's sure another.'

Watching Long Travis manhandling the badly scared Rafe Carter on to his horse, Reilly suddenly became aware of a figure standing next to him. He turned, hand negligently dropping gunwards only to halt as he caught sight of the tarnished metal badge pinned to the sagging vest of a big man only just approaching late middle age.

For a moment, their eyes locked and then the marshal was smiling and extending a broad, iron-hard hand.

'Reilly, ain't it? I'm Bud Defoe, town marshal and county sheriff rolled into one and I'm tellin' you, the job sure ain't no cinch,' the official offered whimsically.

'I heard about you from ol' Eustace,' Defoe went on, 'an' since I knew young Rafe was in town, figgered I'd come along and take care o' any trouble. Looks like you saved me the bother,' he added, examining Reilly judiciously.

'Oh, it weren't no bother, Marshal,' Reilly assured him. 'Kid just needed a little straightening out.'

'Sure,' Defoe nodded, 'young Rafe's had a whippin' comin' for a good long time. Seems like you was as good a man as any to hand it to him.'

'It didn't take much doin',' Reilly offered deprecatingly. 'I figger a ten-year-old kid who ain't missed too many meals could have handled him an' not even have got her dress dirty.'

'It ain't him you're gonna have to worry about,' Defoe informed Reilly bluntly, grinning despite himself. 'By hisself, young Rafe couldn't fight his way out of a pile o' fresh horse shit. But he ain't by hisself and his daddy's money buys him a lot of friends.'

'Nice to have friends,' Reilly said equably, 'although it sure seems like a long time since I had one.'

'Well, o' course,' the Marshal responded, 'I ain't actually your friend but I sure got some friendly advice for you. Quit your job, fork that li'l pinto o' yours and get out of town. And, oh,' he added, apparently struck by an afterthought, 'don't come back . . . ever!'

'Oh no,' Reilly demurred, gently massaging the fingers of his gun hand, 'I figger on stayin'. Things look like they might get right interestin'. Besides,' Reilly muttered to himself as he turned away, 'I'm sure wonderin' what that little bastard meant by "the rest of the valley".'

CHAPTER FOUR

For several long moments after Reilly had left him, Defoe remained staring broodingly after the lone figure. Then, apparently making up his mind, he turned on his heel and made his way to the small cantina where Reilly had rented a room.

'*Buenos dias*, Miguel.' Defoe greeted the owner of the tiny establishment affably. Without preamble, he went on, in his easy border Spanish.

'The gringo, *amigo*, the one who stays here. What is his room?' In a moment, he had the key and was turning to go, when Miguel Ortez, the small, neatly dressed owner of the cantina stopped him.

'What has he done?'

'Why, I don't know, mebbe nothing,' Defoe answered truthfully.

'Then, if your friend is so innocent, Señor Bud, why did he go out so early this morning and come back with his bedroll over his arm?'

For a moment, Defoe perused his friend.

'I don't know,' he answered eventually.' Mebbe I'll ask him.'

Defoe was sitting on the shady porch outside his office later that day as Reilly returned to the cantina after his first day as a newspaper man and the cowboy turned gratefully in answer to the Marshal's shout and inevitable gesture.

'Got a bottle keepin' the desk cool inside,' Defoe offered conspiratorially. 'Care for a spot?'

'Sure would,' Reilly growled through a suddenly tightening throat. 'Just as long as it ain't water . . . or ink!'

'Ol' Eustace workin' you hard?' Defoe began conversationally.

'Well, it ain't quite the same as a calf roundup,' Reilly admitted, flexing his fingers, 'but my head aches from trying to make out them little letters and I sure wish I'd been a better speller at school!'

Defoe grinned and, after the first edge had been taken off his visitor's thirst, he said, 'You're an interestin' fella, Mr Reilly.

'In fact,' the marshal went on, sliding his hand carefully out of sight under the desk where it gripped the worn butt of his six-gun, 'I figgered you was so interestin' that I searched your room, over at Miguel's, today.'

'Figgered you would,' Reilly returned equably, 'it was your most obvious next move. So, tell me, Marshal, what did you find?'

'Nothin' much,' the older man admitted, 'but there was one little thing that bothered me. I can understand a man who ain't got much use for a belt gun, even if he's as good with one as you, owning that old Remington. Makes sense, mebbe, if the feller

31

only uses a gun for varmints and such.'

'But . . .' Reilly prompted, although he could almost guess what was coming.

'But . . . what I can't understand,' Defoe went on, 'is why that same man would have a .45/70 Winchester with custom sights. That looks to me like it fires a special government cartridge. Man who totes a weapon like that,' Defoe concluded, 'waal . . . he tends to have a use for it.'

For a moment, the two men studied each other, then Defoe said, 'Anything you'd care to let me in on?'

'Guess I better let you in on all of it.' Reilly began slowly, mind racing as he worked out exactly how much he dare leave out while still retaining enough to enlist the marshal's aid. Clearly, Defoe could only be a useful ally.

'I come south,' Reilly began slowly, 'looking for a friend o' mine by the name o' Hiram Corcoran.' He caught the momentary flicker in Defoe's eyes. 'He's an engineer, works for the federal governor's office, surveying and such.

'He got sent down here,' Reilly went on, ' 'cause some farmer got het up about an irrigation scheme he had in mind for his farm.'

'You got a name for this farmer?' Defoe interrupted.

'Nope,' Reilly admitted. 'Me and Hymie went mining together a few years back, afore he took this federal job, and his wife telegraphed me and asked if I could come down and find him on account o' her not hearing from him for a coupla months. So here

I am.' Reilly finished.

Without answering, Defoe twisted his chair and eased his spurless heels up on to the battered desk. He squirmed comfortably into his seat and for several long seconds appeared to be gazing vacantly out of the window.

'Just where exactly were you workin' when you got this telegram?' Defoe demanded suddenly, snapping his gaze away from the window to glare at Reilly.

'Why . . . up around El Paso,' Reilly returned, with what he hoped was the right amount of innocent hesitation.

'And Corcoran's wife just happened to know you was there, and that you'd drop everything and head south on her say so. What was you doin' up around El Paso?' Defoe snapped.

'Like always,' Reilly answered with a grin, 'just the very best I could!'

'Listen, Marshal,' Reilly went on before the other could answer, 'I know my story's as full o' holes as a skillet, but you can take it from me, I am looking for Hymie Corcoran and I ain't wanted nor on the dodge. But,' he went on frankly, 'I could sure use some help.'

'OK,' Defoe answered grudgingly, 'what d'you need?'

'Information,' came the brisk retort, 'Did Corcoran get here?'

'Sure,' Defoe answered frankly, 'turned up about six months ago, with a letter from Raoul Sanchez. Letter was asking for federal money to run water across that worthless piece o' dirt he calls a sheep farm. Had some idea he could turn it into the Garden of Eden.' he laughed uneasily.

'Ol' Raoul's a good friend o' mine,' Defoe went on, 'but you sure don't want to start him talkin' about that place o' his.

'Last I saw o' your *amigo*,' the marshal admitted. 'he was headin' towards Raoul's place, across the mountains. Had a load o' camp gear on a pack horse and asked me to keep my mouth shut about who he was.'

'Anything else?' Reilly prompted when his companion seemed reluctant to continue.

'Well, I guess you got a right to know,' Defoe answered reluctantly. 'About two weeks after he left, the ridin' horse he was usin' came back. Coupla days later, so did the pack horse. I took out a search party, but you could lose a coupla armies in them mountains and not notice. Lot of places up there, a fella could be lyin' unconscious a coupla feet away from you and you'd never know it.'

'Anybody else hear him tell you about the Sanchez place?' Reilly asked brusquely.

'I don't think so,' Defoe shook his head doubtfully. 'Mebbe Will was here. That's Will Sovereign, my deppity,' he explained briefly, seeing Reilly's uncomprehending look.

'Oh, and Ansel woulda been here. Ansel Raikes, he's the jailor,' Defoe finished as a tall, cadaverously thin youth, dressed in a worn-out and very dirty town suit, slouched through a rear door which obviously led to an area partitioned off for cells.

'Ansel, you remember that government man come

around here a few months ago?' Defoe asked slowly.

'Remember a fella,' Raikes slurred, 'didn't know he was no gov'ment man. If you say so, Sheriff, I guess he was. I got to get to my chores.' Raikes turned and slouched back into the rear but not before Reilly had noted both a gleam of interest in the man's dull eyes and the bump of a shoulder holster under his coat.

'He's kinda slow,' Defoe said quietly, clearly concerned that the jailor didn't hear him, 'but he's a good worker and we never have anyone dangerous back there.'

'Sure,' Reilly acknowledged thoughtfully. 'What's the story on these Diablos Grafton was tellin' me about?'

'Gang o' murderin' cut-throats is the short answer,' Defoe replied. 'They've terrorized the whole county and some beyond. Driven out a lot of the nesters who settled along the Wahoo and was doin' OK until them varmints showed up. Killed and robbed any number of folks. Wear a red bandanna, coverin' the whole o' their faces, when they're out workin'.'

'Carter bought up them nester farms, according to Grafton,' Reilly remarked.

'Sure,' Defoe admitted, 'and, afore you ask, the trouble with them renegades started about a year before Carter got here.'

'Huh,' Reilly sniffed, 'that don't mean nothin'. Any big time operator'd be sure to fix it so's he didn't look connected with the gang workin' for him. What was the first place he bought?'

'Old man Hennessey's ranch. Heirs sold it to Carter after the old man was bushwacked ... we never did even get a sniff o' who ... done ... it,' Defoe finished slowly.

'Know what Carter paid for it?' Reilly asked casually.

'Hennessey's daughter, who was his only relative, lived back East,' Defoe answered, leaning back in his chair and glaring at his visitor. 'Bank sold the place for her by private auction and talk goes that Carter was the only bid, on account of no one else wanting to deal with them Diablos. And all of a sudden you're startin' to talk a hell of a lot like a lawman, Mr Reilly,' he finished.

'I'm hungry,' Reilly responded inconsequentially. 'Where's the best place to eat in town, Marshal?'

'Good steaks at the Long Branch,' Defoe offered, as Reilly carefully placed his half empty glass on the desk, picked up his hat and rose to go.

At the door, he turned.

'Any place around here that folks generally call "the valley"?' he asked.

'Sure,' Defoe responded. 'Most folks call the Sanchez place that, on account of it is one,' he finished facetiously, before adding as an afterthought, 'Why?' But his only answer was the closing of the door.

And at the back door of the jail, a shadowy figure was saying to Rafe Carter, 'He knows about the Sanchez place. . . .'

'Hey, mister,' a not unfriendly voice called as Reilly

36

pushed through the batwings of Carter's Long Branch saloon and stepped carefully to one side, keeping the wall at his back.

He followed the sound of the voice and found Long Travis propping up the near end of the long polished bar whilst trying to light a cheap cigar.

He was having trouble getting both match and cigar to co-operate and the collection of glasses in front of the tall cowboy provided good reason for his lack of co-ordination.

'Ha' a drink, *amigo*,' Travis slurred, although Reilly's quick eye noticed that the sawdust at the cowboy's feet seemed unusually damp so early in the evening.

'Naw, let me buy you one,' Reilly responded, moving up to the bar and signalling to the bartender.

'Now that's right nice o' you, mister . . .' Travis began when a sneering voice snapped at them.

'Saddle bums ain't allowed in here with decent folks! Ain't that right, boys?'

Reilly sighed gustily. Resignedly, he turned away from the bar to see Rafe Carter standing just inside the batwings. Behind him stood four grinning youngsters of about his own age, cowhands by their dress. One, the biggest, was idly caressing his knuckles.

'Fine,' Reilly returned, sensing, rather than seeing, a suddenly very sober Long Travis moving away from the bar, 'I'll get a drink and a steak somewheres else then.'

'Sure,' Carter acknowledged moving to within arm's length of Reilly, 'after the boys and me have taught you a little respect!'

Level with his last word, Carter swung an awkward punch. Only Reilly wasn't there.

Stepping smoothly to one side, Reilly ducked under the flailing arm, caught the younger man by the neck, jerking him forward and ramming a knee into his stomach.

Carter collapsed on to his knees, gurgling and wheezing, This stopped abruptly as Reilly's knee slammed into his face, smashing his nose to jam and depositing him, senseless, on the dirty floor.

Momentarily, his companions could only stare, shocked into silence by the ruthless efficiency with which their leader had been dealt with. Unconcernedly, Reilly spread his hands.

'Anyone else?' he demanded mildly.

CHAPTER FIVE

'You only had to ask!' the big, chunky young cowboy leading the group assured Reilly, before plunging at him with both hands outstretched.

Reilly, long experienced in bar-room fights, did what the big youngster was least expecting. He stepped quickly between the descending hands, grabbed his opponent's ears and smashed his head squarely across the other's nose.

An agonized scream broke from the unfortunate cowboy's lips as, simultaneously, his nose erupted into a crimson fountain. Grabbing at his severely abused nasal organ, he made the mistake of forgetting all about Fargo Reilly.

He soon remembered, however, as Reilly's foot lashed upwards, catching him between the legs and bringing him to his knees where Reilly's boot, smashing in under his jaw, rendered him indifferent to wordly cares.

Almost by instinct, Reilly twisted and the knife in the hands of the third man missed by a whisker instead of puncturing a kidney, as its owner had intended. Involuntarily, Reilly jerked back, stepping away from his attacker.

He saw the man, a Mexican, draw back his weapon for the killing blow, only to find the knife wrist imprisoned from behind in a vice-like grip as a voice, rich with the blue grass of Kentucky, drawled, 'Now, Pedro, you know it ain't nice to play with knives.'

The owner of the voice, a little man, almost as broad as he was tall, with the scarred, broken-nosed face of a horse breaker, twisted the arm backwards and as the Mexican desperately tried to jerk away, the little man's hand moved in a flickering blur and suddenly there was a Colt in it, the muzzle smashing between the Mexican's eyes. The knife man dropped to his knees and the Colt descended again ruthlessly, laying the man out cold at his attacker's feet.

Desperately, Reilly jerked round, intent upon dealing with the remaining cowboys, only to find them sprawled across the floor and Long Travis blowing on a scarred knuckle.

'What kept you, Dusty, you goddam li'l runt?' the tall one demanded peevishly, clearly addressing Pedro's assailant. 'I sure allus end up havin' to do most o' your goddam work for you!'

'Shet your mouth, you goddam stringbean,' the other responded. 'You ain't never worked a day in your life an' you know it. An' if you don't put your hands back on that table, Billy Kronos, you pig-faced bastard, I'm gonna let daylight through you,' the little man finished, without even a pause for breath.

The man addressed, a cowhand by his clothes, instinctively jerked his hands upwards, his face assuming a mask of savage fury.

'Goddam you, Rhodes, one o' these days you're gonna go too far.'

'Yeah, but not today, Billy boy,' the little horse breaker purred, 'an' anyway, the odds probably don't suit you. After all,' he finished, fluidly palming his second Colt and backing through the door of the saloon, as Reilly and Long Travis joined him, 'I'm lookin' at you, ain't I?'

'Sure sorry you boys lost your jobs, just on account of helpin' me,' Reilly offered, after the introductions had been completed.

Reilly and his companions were sitting in Miguel Ortez's little cantina, where Travis and his companion, Dusty Rhodes, seemed to be well known.

'What makes you think that?' Travis inquired, from around the rim of his beer glass.

'Oh, just little things like, not jumpin' me or lettin' it be done when I beat up young Carter and then kickin' hell outta four o' his boys when they tried to do it,' Reilly explained mildly.

'Oh that!' Travis exclaimed. 'Don't pay no never mind to that! We're breakin' hosses for Carter on contract. . . .'

'Least, I'm breakin' horses,' Rhodes interrupted. 'Long, as usual, is mostly sittin' on the fence, givin' me the benefit o' his advice and opinions.'

'Which you sure need,' Travis snapped. 'Now don't interrupt while the grown ups is talkin'. Like I was trying to say, Carter don't care what goes on in the bunkhouse as long as he gets his money's worth. He's got a rough string out to the Circle C . . . only some of 'em found that they ain't rough enough when they tried a little hoorowing on the runt and me.'

'We'll just head on back, come sun up,' Rhodes stated, 'and that'll be that. We're about finished with his remuda, anyhow.'

'The marshal,' Reilly began, after the boys had acknowledged the greeting of a bow-legged little Mexican, who looked old enough to have come over with Cortez, 'tells me that the high country is some dangerous in these parts. Seems like you two been around here a while. What d'you think?'

'You can't walk more'n a mile, any place up there, without runnin' into a stream, and you can't lose your way, unless you're stupid, 'cause if you just keep walkin' downhill you're bound to cut the old wagon road, which goes to town one way and the Sanchez place the other,' Rhodes summarized, after a glance at his friend.

'Why'd Defoe tell me they was so dangerous then?' Reilly wondered aloud.

'Bud Defoe's honest and a good lawman, as long as he don't have to sit a horse,' Travis snorted. 'He's another one o' them eastern farm boys, come to the grass country to make their fortune, who can't tell a bull from a steer, even when the sign's swingin' in the breeze. An' he hadn't even seen hill country 'til he come here, so naturally same bothers him some.'

'I wouldn't ha' thought this was a place for farm boys, Reilly offered thoughtfully.

'Hell,' Travis snapped irritably, 'they're comin' out o' the woodwork. Why, Lucas Carter, the big mosshead hisself, ain't nothin' but a dirt farmer. Way I hear it, he made a pile o' money sellin' his farm, an' a coupla others, to the railroad after the war.'

'Where would that've been?' Reilly asked casually, aware that another piece of the jigsaw that was form- ing in his head might be about to slip into place.

'Kansas–Missouri border, way I heard it,' Rhodes offered softly.

'Redlegs,' Reilly breathed thoughtfully, 'just the fellas you'd want.'

Aloud, he said, 'Listen fellas, when you get through with them li'l pets o' Carter's, look me up. I've got a li'l job for you.'

Next morning, dawn found Reilly in the saddle and pushing Pecos towards the low range of hills that bordered Raoul Sanchez's valley. He had obtained both directions to the Sanchez place and a holiday from his employer with remarkably little trouble, Grafton's only remark being, 'Bud tol' me you might have business there.'

Barely two hours' ride brought him to a wide, well rutted wagon road that led up through the foothills. As he followed the road, climbing gently, the barren rock soon gave way to pine forest and it was barely noon when he drew rein on the brow of the last hill and looked down the gentle slope that meandered away into the distance, its end marked by a group of dazzlingly white houses from which drifted a welcom- ing column of blue wood-smoke.

Reilly turned his pony's head aside and finding a little clearing, hidden from the road, he stripped

Pecos of his tack and allowed the tough little mustang the luxury of a dust bath, before leaving him to graze on the end of his long picket rope. He might need the strength and staying power in that scarred little body before this job was ended, though, cowboy-like, he invariably took better care of Pecos than he did of himself.

Back at the rim rock, Reilly cradled his heavy calibre Winchester and began to make a cursory survey of the valley.

Sanchez had picked a good spot for the house, easy to defend and snug in winter with good access to the river, which flowed very nearly through the centre of the valley, close to the buildings. But, clearly, the Marshal had been right about the place.

Summer had barely begun, this high up, but the grass was yellowing fast, making poor forage even for the few hardy sheep that dotted the sloping hills.

'Hell,' Reilly offered out loud, 'they can't even be makin' enough to starve on.' Then he stiffened, throwing himself behind a nearby tree and easing back the hammer of his rifle, as the jingle of harness broke the afternoon stillness.

Moments later, a pretty palomino mare walked out of the trees near the road. There was no rider visible but as Reilly tensed, ready to throw lead at anything moving in the trees, a cultured Mexican voice spoke from somewhere in the region of the pony's worn saddle.

'Put down your gun, *señor*,' it said, and as the voice's owner, a slim young Mexican, swung gracefully back into the saddle from where he had been hanging, Comanche style, on the side away from Reilly, the cowboy heard a familiar double click behind him.

Reilly raised his hands in disgust at his own care-lessness as another voice said matter-of-factly, 'It is a bad mistake to spend too much of your time looking only one way, *amigo*.'

'It is true that your friend, Señor Corcoran, came here, some months ago,' Raoul Sanchez admitted easily, as he and Reilly sat over an after-dinner cigar later that night.

Reilly's capture had proved only a temporary embarrassment, eased further when Diego Morales, the Sanchez *segundo* and Reilly's captor, turned out to be the same little bow-legged *vaquero* who had greeted Long and Dusty in the Ortez cantina the night before.

'But these mountains,' the rancher went on, 'they are very dangerous for a, how you say, tenderfeet. Easy to get lost in so that you can never find your way out.' Reilly nodded, pondering this new develop-ment. Sanchez was directly contradicting what Rhodes had told him and what he, Reilly, had seen with his own eyes, following the trail up.

Sure, mebbe in winter, in a bad snow fall, a man could die here, but not in the height of summer and certainly not someone like Hymie Corcoran, who'd cut his teeth surveying the iron road through the Sierra Madres.

'Well, I'm sure you're right, Señor Sanchez,' Reilly lied, 'but I guess I'll just look around anyways, if that's all right?'

'But certainly. You must stay tonight as our guest and in the morning, I will show you the way myself.' But behind the courteous acquiescence, Reilly sensed a tension that sent him towards the bunkhouse in a thoughtful mood.

Later that evening, Reilly wandered down to the horse corral, intent on giving Pecos his nightly sugar. The little pony whinnied his welcome, as Reilly ducked through the bars, and pushed a knowing muzzle towards the pocket of his master's worn chaps.

'Gwan, you ol' reprobate,' Reilly said, gently pushing his mount away, 'I ain't got none tonight.'

With a sly flick, Pecos batted Reilly's worn Stetson off his head and as the cowboy bent to retrieve it, Pecos nudged him sprawling into the dust.

'You win, as usual, *amigo*,' Reilly conceded ruefully as he climbed to his feet.

'He is knowing, that little one,' a voice said from the darkness, as Pecos daintily accepted his nightly treat. Over his shoulder, Reilly saw the figure of the Sanchez *segundo*.

'He sure is,' the cowboy admitted, returning the other's grin and patting his pony's freshly curried neck.

Leaving a contented Pecos, the two men trudged back towards the light of the bunkhouse.

'Don Raoul, he has asked me to show you where your friend, the Señor Corcoran, went up into the hills,' Morales began abruptly.

'I'm pleased,' said Reilly frankly, who was wondering why the rancher had changed his mind about going himself. 'I don't want to get caught looking one way again.' Morales chuckled into the darkness and Reilly went on, 'When the gringo got lost, *amigo*, did you search for him from here?'

'Of course,' Morales asserted, perhaps a shade too vehemently, 'but he was hard to track, *señor*.'

'Looked fairly easy to me, through them pine woods. Ground'd hold tracks a long while, even after the rain.'

'But he did not go up through the pines, *señor*, he went down towards the canyon . . .' Morales began, before stopping abruptly.

'The canyon,' Reilly snapped, 'you mean where the river leaves the valley? Did you know why he was here?' he demanded as an afterthought.

'Sure,' Morales shrugged. 'He come from the governor to tell the boss how we gonna get water on to the land. Make this place the biggest goddam farm in the state!'

'So why in hell did your boss tell me . . .' Reilly began, when the sudden staccato rattle of gun fire split the night.

Instantly lights flared in the main house and Morales had turned, bellowing at the hands tumbling out of the bunkhouse.

'*Los caballos, muchachos.* Get your horses. Those bastards are after the sheep again.'

CHAPTER SIX

Minutes later, Reilly found himself in the saddle and urging Pecos up a well marked trail behind a hard-riding Raoul Sanchez.

Reilly eased up next to Morales, riding hard behind his boss.

'Rustlers, *amigo*?' he bellowed, most of the cry lost in the wind of his pony's speed.

'No,' the other replied, the words whipping savagely past him. 'Better if it were!'

Within seconds, Reilly understood.

As the group thundered over a shallow rise, he looked down becoming aware of a white blot in the distance, which began to take on shape and form as they galloped towards it. Dimly, Reilly could make out the muzzle flashes of the attackers and here and there an answering shot from the herders' weapons.

Suddenly, Pecos bunched and Reilly was almost thrown from the saddle as the little mustang cat-jumped over an object in his path. Only his cowboy's instincts and the iron muscles which years in the saddle had given him, saved Reilly from a fall and certain death.

With a savage curse, he twisted in the saddle, to catch sight of a white bundle, instantly lost to view under the racing hoofs following him.

He turned back, leaning over Pecos's straining neck, suddenly aware that the ground was littered with these objects, like snow drifts suddenly deposited out of a clear blue sky. Then realization struck. Sheep! They weren't stealing the animals, they were simply slaughtering them in a wanton orgy of killing.

Looking up, trusting to his mount's good sense and sure-footedness, Reilly could see the flock rapidly getting closer.

One swift glance took in the situation, then he was easing the racing Pecos around, across the front of the *vaqueros'* hammering ponies and up the gentle slope away from the sheep.

In seconds, Reilly reached his objective and as the ranch crew thundered towards their stock, the night riders turned almost as one man and spurred their mounts into the darkness.

But they had reckoned without Reilly. From his vantage point and with the moon behind him, the riders made a near perfect target as the cowboy unbooted his Winchester, cocked the hammer, sighted and fired in a single flowing movement.

With ruthless precision, Reilly emptied the heavy calibre weapon in the direction of the fleeing badmen, giving a grunt of satisfaction as he saw two of them tumble from their saddles.

And below him, in the dip of ground occupied by

part of the flock. Raoul Sanchez looked up at the formidable figure doing such execution to the killers of his sheep and smiled grimly as he took carefully aim at the man who was trying to save his stock.

But before Sanchez could squeeze the trigger, an apparently chance shot from out of the darkness slammed into his chest, knocking him from his mount and killing him instantly.

That was how his son Luis found him, as a bitter dawn clouded the sky with heat and the Sanchez *vaqueros* gathered what was left from the night's slaughter.

'*Madre de Dios.*' Diego Montoya swore foully and shook his fist in the direction of the sprawling Carter ranch. 'Half the flock dead or crippled, the ewes in lamb, *que malo*,' he paused and a sob escaped his tight set lips, 'and *el patron*, shot like a dog.'

' Sure tough,' Reilly admitted, looking hard at the slope of ground where the dead man lay, sprawled next to his patient mount.

A number of interesting questions were swirling in Reilly's mind.

Such as: why had Sanchez stopped in that particular spot, just below the position, he, Reilly had been occupying? And why did the tracks of his mount show he had been pointing up the slope towards Reilly, when the outlaws were fleeing in the opposite direction? And why had he stopped, anyway?

Reilly had a solution he didn't like which answered all these questions neatly. Except it left the one big question.

Why in hell did Raoul Sanchez want him dead?

'Best you get your boss down to the undertaker's. Diego, *amigo*,' Reilly offered mildly, pulling Pecos to a halt and swinging down in front of the familiar clapboard building that housed Bud Defoe's office.

Seeing the dubious look on the seamed brown face, he added, 'I'll see the marshal with Luis and the *señorita*, if that's OK?'

'*Sí, amigo*,' the little *vaquero* nodded, relief plain in his words. 'Maybe it would be better if you are with Don Luis when he talks to the gringo marshal.'

It was late afternoon on the second day following Raoul Sanchez's death. Reilly had suggested he remain and accompany the family to town and his offer had been gratefully accepted by Luis Sanchez, the dead man's son and the youth who had tricked Reilly so neatly at their first meeting on the ridge above the ranch.

'Diego, *compadre*, there are Carter men in town,' the young man stated, pointing towards the crowded hitching rack outside the town's largest saloon.

'I want no gun play,' he went on softly, but there was the steel of absolute authority behind his words, 'My father would wish no man to throw his life away and it is my wish, too. You will see to this, *compadres*? For me and for the memory of Don Raoul, eh?'

'*Sí, Patron*.' Morales answered, mirroring the nods and muttered responses of his crew. Without another word, Sanchez turned to help his younger sister, Consuela, from the buggy containing the body and then accompanied by Reilly, mounted the steps of the veranda.

'*Patron*, eh,' Reilly muttered to himself. 'I'm sayin' mebbe he is at that.'

They found Defoe seated behind his desk, examining a dog-eared collection of Wanted posters. He seemed oblivious to his visitors, so after a few seconds. Reilly said mildly, 'I ain't there, Marshal, if'n that's who you're lookin' for.'

'It ain't,' Defoe snapped, before looking up and swiftly rising to his feet.

'Heard about your trouble, Luis,' he began without preamble, while swiftly fetching the girl a chair. 'Any idea who it was?'

'You know as well as I do, Marshal, who it was!' the boy snapped, his iron control slipping for a moment. Then it was back and he was saying with a mirthless grin, 'But, like you always say, knowing isn't proving!'

An hour later, their business with the marshal concluded, Reilly led the way out on to the porch again.

'I'll look in at the undertaker's, see how long it'll be 'til your pa's ready to go home,' the cowboy offered.

'*Gracias*, Señor Reilly,' Sanchez answered gratefully, while his sister looked her thanks. 'I will take Consuela to Señora Ortez. She and our mother are old friends.'

The undertaker's, like all such Western establishments, smelled of formalin and dust, in about equal quantities, with something else lurking in the background about which it was probably best not to inquire. The proprietor, a small Chinese of indeterminate age, came from the rear of the shop at Reilly's call.

'Fella just been brought in here,' Reilly began conversationally, 'You know him?'

'Of course I know him,' came the surprising reply, in accentless English. 'Everyone in town knows Señor Sanchez.'

'I'd like for you to do something for me.' Reilly went on carefully, 'When you start workin' on him, see if you can get the bullet out, will you?'

'And just who in hell might you be?' the little man demanded. Reilly introduced himself with a grin and an offered hand, which the other took in a steel-fingered grip, while saying, 'I'm Chin, Lee Chin and do you have any reason for what you ask, apart perhaps from morbid curiosity,'

'Sure,' Reilly responded easily, 'But I ain't sayin' what just yet.'

In the best room of the hotel section of the Long Branch saloon, someone else was bemoaning the death of Raoul Sanchez.

'Of all the goddam, lousy, goddam rotten breaks. Why couldn't that greaser bastard have waited just a coupla days before he got shot? Goddam it, he was due to sign the paper tomorrow,' the big man in the expensive broadcloth suit raged incoherently.

' B-b-but Pa,' Rafe Carter stammered fearfully, 'I thought you wanted that old greaser killed.'

'You're a liar,' Lucas Carter responded savagely.

53

'You never thought that, 'cause you ain't got nothing to think with!' Ignoring his cowering offspring, the elder Carter turned to Billy Kronos, the room's only other occupant.

'Where's the Sanchez kid now?' he demanded savagely.

'Around town, I guess,' Kronos answered slowly, wisely not mentioning that Sanchez's killer had acted under his orders.

'I want that kid hoorowed! Understand? I want him pushed into a fight, then you beat him so bad he don't walk straight again!'

'His sister's with him,' Kronos offered carefully.

'Better and better,' came the callous reply, 'that greaser scum think a lot o' their women. Pushin' him into doin' somethin' stupid oughta be plumb easy.'

'Pa,' the younger Carter began fearfully, 'Why don't we just do the deal with Luis that you'd figgered out with his pa?'

'I don't know where in hell you got your brains from but it sure as hell can't have been me,' his father snapped waspishly. 'I did that deal with Raoul Sanchez 'cause there weren't no way I could scare him or push him out. I ain't wastin' 250,000 dollars on a wet-eared kid.

'Before you start on that Sanchez kid,' Carter ordered a waiting Kronos, 'get Leon Wilson up here. I've got a job for our white-livered banker.'

'Sure, boss,' Kronos grinned, 'but he don't like associating with us dirty cowhands.'

'Ask him if he'd rather choose his friends down in Yuma,' came the sneering retort.

*

'Get away from him, you filth,' Reilly heard the strident voice echoing through the still afternoon as he stepped out of the door of Ortez's cantina. Without pause for thought, Reilly leapt aboard Pecos and lifted him into a dead run in the direction of the scream.

Seconds later, the little mustang slammed to a halt in the main street of Verdad de Soleil, in time for Reilly to see Billy Kronos smash a meaty fist into the side of Luis Sanchez's battered face and Consuela Sanchez slash her quirt expertly across Rafe Carter's bloated cheek.

'Hold him still,' Kronos ordered the two men gripping the young man's arms. 'When we finish with him, we'll have us a li'l fun with his sis—'

What he intended for Consuela Sanchez was lost to posterity, because at that moment Pecos's iron hard shoulder slammed into him, knocking him breathless to the ground.

Cat-quick, Pecos turned and his teeth closed on air inches from the face of one of the men holding Sanchez. Jerking back with a frightened cry, he lost his footing and sprawled in the dust.

His companion fared no better, because before he could release his hold on the Mexican, the toe of Reilly's boot slammed under his heart, leaving the man alternately gasping and vomiting in the dust of the street.

Without a glance at his latest victim, Reilly vaulted from the saddle and advanced on Billy Kronos, now struggling uncertainly to his feet, slamming a viciously swung boot under the chin of the second cowboy as he passed him and knocking him backwards into the street, barely conscious.

'Miz Consuela, are you all right?' Reilly demanded as he smashed his first punch into Kronos's face past the dazed foreman's belatedly raised guard.

'*Sí*,' the white-faced girl responded, ignoring a whining Rafe Carter, unable to draw her eyes away from the violence enacted on the street before her.

The Circle C foreman was big and strong, veteran of a hundred bar-room brawls but he was slow too and unable to touch the lean figure of Reilly, who seemed to hover around him, smashing in blow after blow, punches whose strength seemed out of all proportion to his size.

Finally, one punch lanced in under the Circle C man's jaw and he measured his length in the street, to lay battered and unmoving.

Fists cocked, Reilly looked down at the big man he had so soundly thrashed, then his hands dropped to his side and he said mildly, 'Guess you better stick to beatin' up kids and girls, Billy boy. Looks like that's about all you're good for. You can figger you've had your lesson and we're quits now.'

Reilly turned to go, only to halt in mid stride as a voice from the veranda of the nearby Long Branch sneered.

'Mebbe he's had his lesson, but there's quite some you got to learn, stranger.'

CHAPTER SEVEN

Turning towards the owner of the voice, Reilly saw a big man, equal in size to Billy Kronos, surrounded by seven or eight Circle C cowhands. Where Kronos's bulk was mostly muscle, however, this man's figure was turning rapidly to fat. Reilly nodded.

'I reckon you'll be Carter,' he stated flatly.

'Very good,' the other sneered, taking his cigar from his mouth, 'and since you was kind enough to hand my foreman a lesson, my men are gonna return the compliment. Stomp him, boys!'

With a rush, the Circle C men came at Reilly and it might have gone hard with him, when, apparently from nowhere, a bay thunderbolt cannoned into the group, knocking most of them flying.

One of the Circle C men, a short, pock-marked individual, remained on his feet, however, and seeing Reilly's unprotected back turned towards him, he was reaching for his pistol when a skilfully thrown lariat dropped over his head.

Tightening the instant it reached the cowboy's feet, the rope jerked backwards, pulling the man off his feet to land winded and unarmed in the dust. Looking up, the Circle C rider saw a grinning Long Travis, watching him carefully over the muzzle of a cocked .45.

'That's right, Straker, you just sit a spell,' Travis advised, glancing over to where his old-time friend and side partner Dusty Rhodes, whose bay mare had originally scattered the Circle C men, was herding those individuals who could still walk, including an indignant Lucas Carter, back into the Long Branch using a pair of Colt .45s as an added inducement.

'You better go back to your friends, Straker,' Travis ordered softly: 'Oh, and next time I see you tryin' to shoot a man in the back . . . I won't use a rope. Now, git!'

'Looks like that's another one I owe you boys.' Reilly stated flatly, as he raised his glass from one of the spotlessly scrubbed tables in Miguel Ortez's little cantina.

'Oh, forget it,' Travis snapped, clearly embarrassed.

'Sure,' Dusty Rhodes added. 'Just can't stand a set up. Me an' the stringbean bin on the wrong end of too many our own selves. How's the kid?' he asked, skilfully changing the subject.

'Oh, Mrs Miguel and his sister got him upstairs in bed,' Reilly chuckled, using the nickname that Ortez's wife was known under universally. 'The kid can't stand being fussed over, but Mrs Mig says she thinks Billy and his friends sprung a coupla ribs for him, so she's figgerin' on keepin' him in bed a while.'

'She'd sure know,' Rhodes stated flatly. 'You mind that time she took that bullet outta you?' he demanded of Travis, 'better'n a college doctor, I reckon.'

'Sure is,' Travis agreed, contentedly sucking down the contents of his glass and reaching for the bottle. 'And some cheaper.'

'I'm assumin' from the polite way you boys addressed yourselves to friend Carter this afternoon that you ain't working for him no more?'

'Never insult your boss,' Travis informed Reilly seriously, 'at least, not 'til he's paid you,' the tall one finished, complacently patting a bulging pocket.

'So would you boys be lookin' for a job?' Reilly went on mildly.

'Not so you'd notice,' Rhodes answered quickly. 'What kinda job?' the little man demanded suspiciously.

'Oh, nothin' much,' Reilly answered offhandedly, 'just the key to this whole damn business down here. I want you to find where the Diablos are hidin' out.'

'So it looked like it was all tied up neat. Carter seemed like the real crook to me, and the only mistake he'd made was tyin' hisself in with them Diablos.' Reilly explained. 'If anyone can prove a connection, then Carter's done for. That's why I need to know where they're at, 'cause I still think dear Lucas is in this up to his dirty neck.'

'See,' the cowboy went on, 'I figgered Carter probably killed Corcoran to stop him sendin' his report, so's he could buy Sanchez's land for a song. Stands to reason if a government surveyor said it looked good, the old man'd have hung on, come hell or high water.' Reilly finished his explanation as the short Arizona twilight moved towards full dark.

'Sounds like you don't think that now?' Dusty Rhodes offered.

Reilly shook his head, mouth busy with a fresh cigar. 'It sure don't look that simple now,' he agreed.

'Mind tellin' us why?' Rhodes persisted.

'Nope,' Reilly returned, 'It's 'cause, last night, after I told him I was lookin' for Hymie Corcoran, Señor Raoul Sanchez, currently deceased, tried to shoot me.'

Some days later, Reilly was lazily sweeping the porch in front of the *Tribune*'s office, when a rider pulled his mount to a halt in the street next to him.

'*Buenos días*, Señor Reilly,' the rider, Luis Sanchez, greeted him. 'A beautiful day for a ride, no?'

'Does your sister know you're outta bed?' Reilly demanded. 'An' what you doin' ridin' that crow bait?'

'I am well again and women, they like to fuss too much and Señor Ortez lent me his blood horse,' Sanchez explained, indicating the docile little roan he was riding with a graceful sweep of his hand, 'because *mi querida* Bella has a stone bruise.'

'He sure thinks a heap o' that li'l palomino horse,' Reilly mused as he watched Sanchez ride gently up the dusty street. 'Wonder how she hurt her hoof? And I wonder where them two sorry specimens are headin',' he added as he watched Rafe Carter and his friend Karl Straker riding out of town behind the young Mexican.

'Whatfer you gotta cut a hole in my hat fer, Rafe?' Straker whined as he watched the younger Carter at work with a battered Barlow knife.

'You heard what Dad said,' Carter explained wearily. 'You hide out here, an' I take your hat an' pony back in to town, claimin' I found 'em out here near them painted rocks.' He paused, gesturing towards the nearby canyon of the Wahoo, where it flowed from the flat grassland of the Sanchez ranch into the narrow hard rock canyon, which formed the boundary of Carter's Circle C, in a bare mile transformed from a placid mill pond to a death-dealing, raging torrent.

'Then I tell how I backtracked and found where someone had tied a palamino pony to a tree and smoked a coupla them high-falutin' Spanish cigarillos Luis Sanchez likes so much,' he finished with a satisfied smirk.

'And then, when Sanchez comes back from his little ride, Billy makes sure he gets strung up? B-b-but what about Marshal Defoe?' Straker finished.

'Oh, Dad's got that figgered,' Carter assured his friend. 'The marshal's gonna want to look at the evidence hisself. So he'll leave Will Sovereign in charge and Sanchez locked in the jail. Will'll lock hisself in nice and tight, except I happen to know that the back door is gonna accidentally get itself unlocked.' Carter grinned evily. 'It's sure a cinch. Sanchez'll be dead and them women'll have to sell the ranch to Pa. Now, you go and kill me a jack-rabbit or something so's I can bloody up your hat an' saddle.'

Ten minutes later, his preparations complete, Rafe Carter swung aboard his pony and gathered up the reins of Strake's mount, both animals restless and nervous, smelling the blood that coated the latter's saddle.

'Now you just lose yourself for a coupla days, Karl. There's a pony hid back in the brush there,' Carter ordered, 'got grub an' a canteen. Then, when you come back to town, what you gonna say?'

'Whomped on the head while I was ridin' along the canyon, come to, wandered off, near starved in the mountains afore I found the wagon road and remembered who I was,' Straker recited. Carter grimaced.

'Even I wouldn't believe that story,' he sneered, 'but with Luis dead, it won't matter much what you say. *Adios.*'

'Wait up, Rafe,' Straker ordered. 'I need my rifle,' he explained, reaching up and drawing the long-barrelled Sharps from its specially made boot.'

'Can't understand anyone carrying a single shot gun these days,' Carter sneered.

' 'Cause it shoots twice as far as a repeater,' Straker responded, with the easy assurance of an expert. 'An' it come in right handy the other night,' he went on with a self-satisfied nod, cradling his weapon and turning in the direction his borrowed pony lay, 'for sheep and . . . other things.'

Rafe Carter's hoof beats had long since died into the distance before Straker stumbled across the picketed and contentedly grazing pony. With a curse at the stupidity of whoever had hidden the animal, Straker propped his rifle carefully on the piled gear and grabbed at the picket line with a vicious snatch.

Being concerned solely with filling his belly on the sparse herbage in front of him, the pony showed his resentment at having his lawful occupation interrupted by this two-legged nuisance by rearing and showing his teeth. It was nothing more than the sort of display any self-respecting Texas mustang feels he's entitled to before settling down to a day's work, but it incensed Straker, none too stable a personality at the best of times, to the point of madness.

Jerking savagely on the picket line, he forced the pony's head down and flinging back his quirt, aimed a blow at the little mustang.

The cowardly stroke never landed, Straker stopping short as an icy voice said, 'I wouldn't do that, Karl. You're gonna be ridin' that pony to town with your hands tied and he may give you trouble if'n you annoy him.' Meanwhile an object, the shape of which Straker recognized only too well, tried to bore a hole in his left kidney.

Anxiously, knowing that any sudden move would invite a bullet. Straker turned a nervous head to encounter the grinning features of Fargo Reilly, while that gentleman's heavy calibre Winchester caressed the Circle C man's backbone.

'I .. I . . .' Straker began.

'Don't bother lyin',' Reilly interrupted with a grin, although the look on his face held nothing of humour. 'I heard you boys talkin'. Listened to the whole thing.' Seeing the look on Straker's face, Reilly's grin broadened.

'Don't you worry none, son,' he assured the horror-stricken cowboy, 'you can tell the marshal all about it your own self. I'll just be there to kinda . . . jog your memory some. *Comprende*?' he asked, lifting the Winchester significantly. Straker gave a terrified nod.

'Now, you just saddle up and don't get no ideas about that Sharps cannon o' yours.' Reilly backed towards Straker's borrowed riding gear and hefted the heavy rife. 'Wonder what ol' Lee Chin's got to say about the bullet that killed ol' man Sanchez?' he asked of no one in particular.

Back in Verdad, Carter's plan was working smoothly. Much against his will, Bud Defoe had been forced to put Luis Sanchez behind bars. Anger had made him terse as he issued Will Sovereign with his final instructions.

'Lock all the doors and sit facin' the front with a scatter gun on your lap. Don't let no one, and I mean no one, in or out 'til I get back. Oh and tell that wife o' yours not to come by with coffee or cake or nothin'.'

'Hell, Bud,' Sovereign offered with his slow grin, 'I never heered you put up no squawk about Marcie's pound cake afore. I'll tell 'er you ain't partial no more, shall I?'

'Just watch yourself,' was Defoe's only rejoinder as he lugged saddle and rifle through the door.

And Sovereign had obeyed his boss's instructions

religiously, right up until the moment a creaking floorboard had drawn his head around only to have a swiftly-used gun butt lay him on the floor out cold.

With Sovereign dead or disabled, Billy Kronos and a dozen Circle C men had dragged a fighting mad Luis Sanchez from his cell, thrust him roughly up on a horse and led him to the old cottonwood on the outskirts of town and the milling, shouting mob gathered around it.

Stillness settled over the crowd that had gathered to watch as a rope was tossed over a convenient branch of the old tree and settled over the young Mexican's neck. In the back of the crowd, Dusty Rhodes nudged his partner and both men began to work their way out of the press, Rhodes absently loosening his Colts as he walked.

'What about the marshal?' a voice demanded from the back of the crowd, Kronos shrugged burly shoulders.

'He can bitch all he wants,' the Circle C foreman jeered. 'Ain't gonna be much he can do if the kid's dead.'

Turning to Sanchez, Kronos demanded. 'Any last words, kid?'

'Yes, you gringo bastard,' the boy retorted, 'you're a coward and a liar and if you give me a gun for five minutes by the clock I'll kill every damn son of a bi—'

'Shut up, you greaser bastard,' Kronos interrupted, slashing his heavy quirt across the young man's face. Turning to the crowd he began. 'We're here to see justice done for our buddy, Karl Straker,

65

murdered by this yellow greaser son of a—'

'Friend Straker seems a tolerable lively corpse to me,' a mild voice interrupted from the back of the crowd.

CHAPTER EIGHT

Unceremoniously, Pecos shouldered his way through the crowd, teeth bared for anyone who came too close, the Circle C man's horse edging uneasily after the little mustang.

Reaching the group around the cottonwood, Reilly dropped easily out of the saddle and indicated a petrified Karl Straker.

'Like I said,' the cowboy offered, 'he makes a tolerable lively corpse and last time I looked he was still breathing.'

'Sure,' Kronos responded, turning with disarming slowness, 'that's more than you'll be able to say about the greaser!'

Before the last word left his mouth, Kronos sprang towards the pony upon which a relieved Luis Sanchez was sitting and slashed his quirt across the restive animal's rump.

The pony jerked forwards but before the noose could tighten, there was a shattering roar from a nearby doorway, the rope parted with a vicious snap and Long Travis's large, knowledgeable hands were calming Sanchez's' maddened pony, while Dusty Rhodes was urgently pulling the young Mexican from the saddle.

From the doorway of a nearby ruined adobe, Will Sovereign growled, 'I got one barrel left in this here instrument and I'm gonna dish it out regardless, unless I get my prisoner back in that cell now.' Slowly, legs unable to support him any longer, Defoe's deputy slid down the door frame until he subsided, propped against the splintery jamb. But the scatter gun never wavered and there was steel in the voice that snapped, 'I mean it, goddam it, get him over here now.'

'He can't do nothin',' Kronos sneered, reaching surreptitiously for a Colt. 'Get 'im, boys, he ain't—' he began, only to be interrupted by Reilly, who adopted the simple but effective expedient of smashing the barrel of his Remington across the Circle C man's nose.

Kronos screamed as his nose broke again, dropping his pistol and grabbing for his badly damaged features. His pain didn't last long, Reilly savagely pistol-whipping his opponent into unconsciousness with half a dozen swift, savage strokes.

A trance-like silence enveloped the waiting mob as the lean cowboy carefully used Kronos's filthy shirt to wipe the blood thoroughly from the barrel of his gun. Satisfied at last, the weapon twirled absently on Reilly's finger before seeming to slip of its own accord into the battered, greasy holster.

'Anyone else?' Reilly demanded softly, but the crowd was already melting like snow before spring sunshine.

*

'Ol' Bud sure looked mad when he come back and found Carter had sent him on a wild goose chase,' Eustace Grafton chuckled, leaning back and drawing on his after-dinner cigar.

'Not half as mad as he was when he saw what them Circle C boys had done to Will,' Reilly grinned. 'How's Luis?' he asked of no one in particular.

'Oh, stubborn, as usual,' Millie Grafton offered absently, adding, as a quick afterthought, 'at least, so Consuela was telling me.'

A sly grin flicked across Reilly's face as he asked, 'His sister told you, huh?' And as Millie retreated in blushing confusion to the kitchen, ostensibly to tackle the dishes, Grafton lowered his voice and grinned across at Reilly.

'I like that Sanchez boy,' the old man confided. 'He's got the right stuff in him. Feet on the ground too, not like his pa.'

'What d'you mean?' Reilly asked absently, 'Not like his pa?'

'Ol' Raoul was the sort to just roar in, guns blazing if he thought there was a problem needed solving,' Grafton said. 'Luis is more like his ma, thinks afore he acts.' From the corral, a whip-poor-will called softly twice.

'How long you known about them two?' Reilly asked, lowering his voice to a whisper.

'What, you mean the secret signal and meetin' on the porch and such?' Grafton returned. 'Since about the second time the boy turned up here. I was goin'

69

to bed and heard 'em fussin'. And afore you ask,' he went on quickly seeing the question forming on Reilly's lips, 'I ain't said nothin, 'cause I figger when she's ready, she'll tell me. Her grandma was perzactly the same,' the old man finished softly. 'Loved a li'l romance.'

Abruptly, there came a hammering on the street door.

'Now who in hell can that be?' Grafton demanded, rising and stamping across the faded carpet.

'Don't know, Eustace,' Reilly answered slyly. 'Mebbe if'n you opened 'er up, you'd find out.'

'Shut up, you,' Grafton snapped as he savagely twisted the inoffensive door handle. 'One smart alec around here is sure aplenty and I ain't lookin' for no competition.'

Throwing back the door, while still glaring hard at his grinning employee, Grafton revealed a slight, greying man blinking owlishly in the lamplight. He had the pale, slightly puffy face and stooped, rounded shoulders of one who spends his working life indoors although, at that moment, the pale face was puckered into a worried frown.

'Eustace, I need to talk to you.' His quick glance took in Reilly's lounging figure and he added nervously, 'Alone, if you don't mind.'

'Sure, Leon, we'll go into the office. Fargo, this is Leon Wilson, runs the Cattleman's Association Bank.' Reilly nodded and offered his own name, extending a hard hand.

'G-g-glad to know you, Mr Reilly,' Wilson returned, limply returning the cowboy's grip. 'I mean no offence by asking Eustace to talk in private. I hope you understand?'

'Sure,' Reilly answered affably, 'I got some readin' to do, anyhow.'

'Finished up with Mr Wilson?' Reilly asked mildly as Grafton crossed the room, after seeing his visitor out, and stood examining the title of the book Reilly was buried in.

'Agricultural Dynamics,' Grafton read slowly, 'you thinking o' turning to farming, Fargo?'

'Nope,' Reilly responded frankly, 'I'm just diggin' the dirt. Oh and by the way, I'm gonna be takin' another li'l holiday. Startin' tomorrow.'

'Goddam it,' Grafton snarled. 'How'm I supposed to get a paper out when my assistant ain't never here? Where in hell you going?'

'Prospectin',' Reilly answered shortly.

In the shadow thrown by a run down adobe, across the street from Grafton's house, a figure wearing a dirty, worn store suit watched carefully as Leon Wilson made his way home, after leaving the newspaper editor's front door.

With a grunt of satisfaction, Ansel Raikes left his post and turned towards the back door of Carter's saloon. What he had just seen sure ought to be worth something to somebody, he decided.

Early next day, the morning sun tipped sleepily over the horizon to find, once again, a little paint mustang pushing easily along the plain trail out of

Verdad de Soleil. Its rider was Fargo Reilly and he was alternately leading and cursing an unwilling pack mule, an animal which had once been the property of one Hymie Corcoran, federal engineer and surveyor, now missing, believed deceased.

'I never could have much truck with mules, Pecos.' Reilly informed his mount. 'But this one is sure the most God-awful stubborn specimen of the breed I ever had the misfortune to run acrost. Come on, damn you!' he finished, jerking the unwilling animal after him.

Late afternoon found the trio overlooking the valley of the Wahoo, and Reilly dropped gratefully from Pecos's back before securely roping the fractious mule to a substantial tree root.

'First, we gotta find somewheres to start from, Pecos,' Reilly informed the little paint, while dextrously rolling and lighting a smoke. 'An' I guess a spell o' Mrs Sanchez's cooking wouldn't be too hard to bear,'

'Potatoes, lettuce, onions and these,' Maria Sanchez indicated a bunch of tomatoes, the largest of which was nearly as big as Reilly's fist, 'these do best of all.'

'I don't think I've ever seen a finer garden,' Reilly responded and meant it. 'But what about water?'

'That's my big problem. The boys bring it in buckets every day and they all hate to do it,' she confided, dropping her voice. 'But they all like to eat, so they don't say too much. At least not to me,' she finished, with a shy smile.

Reilly had been welcomed enthusiastically at the hacienda and with dinner over, he had asked Maria Sanchez about her vegetable garden, glimpsed momentarily as he rode up. She had offered to show him round and was talking enthusiastically about the seeds she had had from Washington.

'Soil seems pretty good here,' Reilly offered, bending to lift a handful of the black, friable earth, when his companion had paused momentarily for breath. 'Is there much more like this, through the valley, *señora?*' For a moment, Maria Sanchez looked at him in disbelief.

'Señor Reilly, the whole valley is like this,' she answered with a soft laugh, 'that's why the place is called Mesa del Negro.'

'Black Mountain,' Reilly translated softly, 'I see.'

Next day, Reilly was in the saddle early and pushing gently north, with Pecos and a shovel for company.

Noon had come and gone long since, when Reilly slammed his shovel into the pile of earth he had excavated and flopped down beside it and began to roll the inevitable cigarette. Pecos, grazing contentedly at the end of a long picket rope looked up at the noise.

'I hope you're enjoying yourself, *amigo,*' Reilly asked whimsically. 'Blister end of the shovel is sure right,' he added ruefully, looking at his sore, aching hands, 'but, at least, we know now Mrs Sanchez was right. Whole valley's covered in this black soil. Prime farmin' land and hard to come by in this part of the world. All you need is water and it'll be worth a fortune.

'So, if a man owns something like this,' Reilly went on slowly, 'what in hell made Raoul Sanchez take a pot-shot at me? Sure a puzzler,' he finished, slipping Pecos's saddle into place and pulling on the cinch.

'Plain to see Carter's set on takin' over the whole valley, though, and since it's all like this, ain't hard to understand why. Wonder what he'll try next, *amigo?*' Reilly offered as he swung into the saddle and reached down to pick up the shovel.

'Huh, mule tracks,' Reilly grunted, leaning out of the saddle for a closer look, 'and two horses with him. Question is, o' course, whose mule?'

Heading back to the Sanchez hacienda, Reilly had decided to take a look at the area where Diego Morales claimed Corcoran had been heading on his last day. Reaching the placid, even waters of the Wahoo some way below the ranch house, Reilly simply turned towards the mountains and in no time at all found himself climbing a gentle slope composed of some sort of loose and rotting rock, which slipped and moved under his mount's hoofs.

Despairing at last of making further progress safely, Reilly had turned Pecos away from the treacherous river bank and soon found firm ground more to his mount's liking. He'd also found the mule tracks.

Without taking his eyes from the tracks, Reilly backed Pecos away, before dropping the reins over the little mustang's head, ground hitching him as securely as if he'd been tied.

Back at the trail, Reilly knelt down and made a thorough examination of the tracks of all three animals.

'That's sure Hymie's mule,' he assured himself, 'but I ain't never seen the other two. One've 'em must have been a fair piece o' horse though, Pecos,' he informed his mount as he swung aboard the little pony and headed him down the slope towards the Sanchez ranch house. 'Going by the size of his hoofs an' his stride. Guess I'll sure know him again when I see him.'

Evening was falling as Reilly drew rein in front of the main house. Cowboy-like, he eased the girths of the weary little mustang before leading him first to the water trough and then to the barn, well lit by the lantern Morales had plainly left burning for him. The little *segundo* must have heard his hoof-falls because he came from the house just as Reilly led Pecos into a stall and began to fork hay into the manger for his pony.

This done, he picked up the brushes, intending to finish caring for the little pony, but just as Morales stepped through the door, the recalcitrant curry comb leapt from Reilly's hand, and described an arc that left it lying on the straw-covered floor just behind the stall of a big chestnut stallion Reilly had never seen before.

With a sigh, the cowboy stumped over to the brush and bent to lift it from the straw.

Then he froze, because clear in the dust of the

barn, Reilly saw the tracks of the horse which had accompanied Hymie Corcoran's mule on what might have been his owner's last ride.

CHAPTER NINE

'Who does that pretty pony belong to, *amigo*?' Reilly asked, as Morales passed him with a feed bag of oats for a grateful Pecos.

'Hijo, the chestnut, you mean? Don't go near him, *amigo*, the *segundo* warned seriously. 'He was Don Raoul's mount and only *el patron* could handle him. I think mebbe we have to shoot him, he is just too . . . how you say . . . *malo*.'

'Yeah, I know,' Reilly nodded thoughtfully. 'A bad one.'

Sitting at dinner later that evening in the Sanchez hacienda, Reilly found his train of thought, which was revolving around the whereabouts of a certain chestnut stallion on the day Hymie Corcoran disappeared, interrupted, when Luis Sanchez said abruptly, 'Tomorrow, I have to go to town to see Mr Wilson, the banker.'

'But why?' Maria Sanchez demanded quietly, as her son returned to his *mole* sauce.

'His note said only business. To do with the ranch, *Mamasita*. Don't worry, it's probably nothing.' But

Reilly didn't miss the concern in the boy's dark eyes and promptly decided that, interesting though the tracks in the canyon were, the banker's news might well be more important.

'I'll ride along with you, Luis,' he offered quietly. Sanchez nodded, smiling briefly, while his mother smiled gratefully.

'T-t-thank you for coming so promptly, S-S-Señor Sanchez,' Wilson stammered, rising from his desk behind the grill and walking past the counter to meet the young rancher.

'We can talk in private in my office, if you'd care to come this way,' Wilson went on, looking pointedly at Reilly who, after accompanying his young friend to town, had followed him into the bank.

'Fargo, I'll see you at the cantina?' Sanchez began awkwardly.

'Sure,' Reilly assured him, 'Give me a chance to get rid of that goddam mule, anyhow.'

The undertaker's was deserted as Reilly slipped through the door to stand in the dreary dust and formalin-smelling little shop.

Before he could open his mouth, however, there was a swish of bead curtains and the small, compact figure of Lee Chin appeared noiselessly behind the counter.

'It's about that bullet, isn't it?' the little man began without preamble.

'Get anything?' Reilly asked mildly.

The little man shook his head.

'There was an entry wound, like this,' he began, raising a finger to suggest the size of the hole, 'but where the bullet came out was a mess. Took out a piece of rib and muscle the size of my fist.'

'So you couldn't get no idea about what sorta rifle might have done it?' Reilly asked.

'Well, I wouldn't quite go that far, Mr Reilly,' the little man began precisely. 'I can't tell you exactly what caused Señor Sanchez's fatal wound, but I can tell you what didn't.'

'OK,' Reilly shrugged, 'I'm guessin' you're rulin' out any kinda hand gun?'

'Logic would do that already,' the little man admitted, 'from what I heard about the distances involved. And it wasn't a Winchester, least ways, not .44/40 calibre.'

'How in hell can you tell that?' Reilly demanded, suddenly all attention.

'The bullet hit a rib going in,' the little man explained. 'Went clean through the heart, like it wasn't there and tore a fist-sized hole in the victim's back. Takes a good load of powder behind a big bullet to do that, at least in my experience. Especially given that the shooter must have been a couple of hundred yards away.

'And if I was asked to guess,' the little Chinaman went on carefully, 'I'd say it wasn't one of those bigger calibre weapons that fires the government cartridge. No, I think you're looking for something like a Sharps. A buffalo gun,' the little man finished. 'Does that help?' he asked.

'That,' Reilly answered, as he tipped back his hat

in mild vexation and made for the door, 'depends on how many yahoos on this range are ridin' around with one of them miniature cannons for a saddle gun. Thanks, Mr Lee, I'll be seein' you.'

Reilly found Luis Sanchez waiting for him in the cantina.

'Didn't take you very long.' Reilly began carefully, seeing the warning signals in the younger man's drawn brows and firmly compressed lips.

'No,' Sanchez snapped, 'it does not take a gringo banker long to tell a Mexican that soon he will no longer own his land!'

'Best tell it slow,' Reilly offered, ignoring the proffered tequila bottle and settling back in his chair to roll a smoke.

'Señor Wilson has a paper, drawn in my fathers' name for a mortgage of fifty thousand dollars on the ranch. How he intended to pay I don't know,' the young man explained. 'But the paper is due at the end of this month and there is not fifty dollars cash in the whole ranch, apart from the men's wages.'

'Can't you sell stock?' Reilly offered the obvious suggestion.

'Sheep don't sell that easily,' Sanchez admitted. 'Our only buyer is south of the border and he buys only in the winter, when we can drive without losing the whole flock. Try to move sheep any distance in this heat,' Sanchez finished, 'and you'd lose most of them. Besides, at this time of year, every water hole between here and Casa Verde will be dry.'

'Won't he wait 'til shippin' time?' Reilly asked.

'Señor Wilson says the bank is over extended on its loans and he needs the money. I got the feeling, though,' the young man added thoughtfully, 'that he wasn't any happier about it than I was.'

'Like someone was pushin' him into it?' Reilly asked.

'Mebbe,' the young man shrugged, 'I don't know. But it makes no difference,' he added miserably. 'Either I sell the ranch myself or lose it.'

'Wilson happen to mention if he had a buyer lined up?' Reilly asked absently.

'Sure,' Sanchez admitted bitterly, 'I bet you can't guess who.'

'Name wouldn't begin with Lucas and end in Carter, would it?' Reilly asked helpfully.

At that precise moment, the object of their discussion was conducting some business of his own with a less than co-operative employee.

'I'm just saying it's not the safe way to play this, Mr Carter,' Leon Wilson whined. 'It isn't the same as giving you information about those farmers' bank accounts. I could go to prison. . . .'

'Well, you won't have to worry none about that, Wilson or mebbe I should say, Hargreaves,' Carter paused, as the banker's face whitened. 'That little gal in Coronado never did get over the little game you played that night and if the *rurales* ever found out . . .' he paused, revelling in his ability to cause suffering.

'Anyhow, things like that ain't gonna come up, not unless they got to.' Carter paused again, leaving the threat hanging in the air. 'All you gotta do is go along with what I say and everything'll be sweet. Step outta line, you snivelling, yeller-gutted son of a bitch,' Carter finished with a snarl, 'and you'll swing. Get this, I'm the boss and I don't need your goddam white-livered advice.

'And don't forget to let that greaser kid know about my offer,' Carter ordered, pausing at the door. 'Fifty thousand cash.'

'Goddam your rotten soul.' Wilson shook his fist at the closed door. 'But I'll get you yet,' he raged, teeth drawn back in an uncharacteristic snarl. 'Just see if I don't.'

Outside the closed door, Carter scratched a match and applied it carefully to the end of his cigar. Even rats can bite, came the thought unbidden. Perhaps the Diablos had better pay the town a visit . . . Yes, that might be the best answer all round.

It was in the afternoon two days later, just about first drink time, when a tall, thickset cowhand, sporting a black beard that brushed the front of his shirt and riding a strongly muscled grey gelding, paced sedately down the main street of Verdad de Soleil and pulled his mount roughly to a halt in front of the bank.

He secured the horse to the worn hitching rail with a careful slip knot and, in no apparent hurry, ascended to the veranda, accompanied by two cowboys who had joined him from the street and seemed to have business in the bank too.

Swiftly, the big man examined the street, then he jerked a red bandanna up and over his face. His companions immediately followed his example before all three pushed quickly through the half-glazed door and into the bank.

The last man through the door slammed it shut and lowered the blinds, while the big man snatched out a Colt and growled throatily, 'Get your hands up! This here is a stick-up! Don't do nothin' stupid and nobody gets hurt!'

Two other men, already in the bank, instantly produced pistols, covering the old guard and the teller behind the counter.

'Fill this,' the big man, clearly the gang's leader, snapped. 'Quick. And don't forget the safe.'

'There's nothing in the s-s-safe,' Leon Wilson offered shakily as he rose from his desk and advanced on the man.

'I sure hate a liar,' the big man sneered, firing twice. Hit in the chest, Wilson collapsed without a sound.

'Now you know I ain't jokin' . . . get . . . to . . . that safe,' Wilson's killer demanded and the teller fell over himself in his rush to obey.

'Get your horses, boys!' Bud Defoe yelled through the swinging batwings of the Long Branch saloon. 'The bank's been robbed by them damn Diablos! They're headin' for the hills and we can mebbe catch 'em if we get a goin'.'

There was a general rush for the door, one which Reilly, who was occupying an out of the way seat in the corner near a window that looked on to the main street, didn't join.

He was still there half an hour after the noisy departure of the posse had died into the distance, at which point he rose and sauntered out of the saloon and into the evening twilight.

Momentarily he paused on the boardwalk, thoughtfully rubbing his chin, then turned and ambled away towards the town's largest livery stable.

At the last and smallest of Verdad's horse barns, Reilly found what he was looking for. The big grey with the white patches looked nothing like the horse Wilson's killer had ridden into town but as Reilly ran a hand down the warm flank, he felt the characteristic stickiness and found, not unexpectedly, that his hand was covered in white paint when he drew it away.

'Clever,' he acknowledged, scrubbing his hand through the dust of the floor to remove the paint which had changed the horse's identity. 'Sheriff on a wild-goose chase, while them Diablos sashay off in another direction, calm as you please. Wonder if Long and Dusty had any luck with their huntin'?'

Leaving the barn, Reilly glanced up at the worn board over the big double doors.

'L. Carter, prop, meanin' he owns the place,' Reilly acknowledged to himself. 'Which just about fits the last piece.'

Behind and above him, in the horse-smelling darkness of the ramshackle barn hayloft, the big man who had killed Leon Wilson eased himself silently to the top of a bale of hay and sighted along a noiselessly drawn pistol.

Cursing, because the distance and the angle made the shot impossibly uncertain with a Colt, the big man dropped back, scrabbling at his long black beard and eventually tearing the whole mass of woolly hair from his chin to reveal the reddened and much battered face of Billy Kronos.

Waiting only until Reilly had made his way back down the street, Kronos slipped out of the rear of the stable.

'I tell you he's seen the grey,' Kronos all but gibbered. 'We're gonna have the law on our necks as soon as Defoe gets back!'

'Get Sancho.' Carter ordered, after a moment's thought. 'Greys ain't that uncommon and the greaser can move him out with the rest of the cavvy tonight. If you remember, that was how I figgered to get them ponies outta town anyhow. Sancho'll just have to go sooner than we planned is all.'

'OK,' Kronos acknowledged. 'But what about this cowboy? Seems to me he keeps turnin' up in just exactly the sort of place you don't want him to turn up.'

'He do, don't he,' Carter answered thoughtfully. 'Mebbe we should do something about Mister Nosey Parker Reilly at that.'

'Get yourself down to the depot. Billy boy,' Carter ordered playfully. 'Send a message to Fort Craig. Ask Lane Walker how he'd like to make five thousand dollars.'

CHAPTER TEN

'Are you sure running this story about the Diablos and how Carter's mixed up with them is a good idea, Grandpa?' Millie Grafton asked dubiously as she scanned the latest edition of the *Verdad Tribune*.

'I ain't mentioned Carter by name, all I said is certain vested land interests seem to benefit unreasonably by the actions of these desperados,' Grafton objected.

'What d'you think, Fargo?' the old man demanded of his assistant. Reilly's reply was eloquent.

He simply rose, took down his battered gun belt from its hook by the door and buckled it on, carefully tying down the holster bottom.

'Answer your question?' he asked, absently checking the shells in the Remington cylinder.

As it happened, the subject of Grafton's editorial called that morning with a copy of the paper clutched in his fist and if the old man's story had caused him any annoyance, Carter was careful not to show it.

'Morning Grafton, Miz Millie,' he began affably enough, touching his hat to the girl and ignoring Reilly. 'Fine piece in today's paper about them Diablo skunks,' he complimented. 'Can't have these damn bandits murderin' respected citizens like that.'

'Wilson ain't dead,' Reilly offered mildly. 'Mrs Ortez says he's more'n likely to live.'

Give him his due, Reilly admitted, watching Carter visibly digest the news, which must have been a shock and could easily spell disaster for his carefully laid plans, he don't give much away.

'Why, that's fine,' Carter responded expansively. 'Wilson's a fine businessman, always been an asset to the town. But it don't change what I come to see you about, Grafton.'

'You mean this ain't just a social call,' the old man returned waspishly. 'Shucks, Lucas, you don't know how disappointed I am about that.'

Reilly, who had gathered up the almost bristleless office broom and was idly rearranging the dust on the floor as an alternative to sweeping it, as well as an excuse to stay and hear what Carter wanted, hid a grin behind his calloused hand.

'Well, always glad to call on a fellow businessman,' Carter boomed pompously, apparently immune to sarcasm. Only the glitter behind his eyes betrayed him as he continued.

'I want to run this notice in the *Tribune*, full page spread, no expense spared.'

Accepting the piece of paper, Grafton scanned it and his eyes widened with shock, because the notice said:

TO WHOM IT MAY CONCERN

I, Lucas Carter, give notice that I am taking over the bank of Verdad, with all its assets and debts, and will make good all losses incurred in the recent robbery, dollar for dollar. No depositor will lose a dime.

Date of reopening to be announced.

Reilly looked up from where he was reading over Grafton's shoulder.

'All assets and debts?' he asked.

'Sure,' Carter sneered, 'and since this business has left me tolerable short of cash, I'll be callin' in mortgages as soon as the deal's gone through. And the first I'll be callin' will be on that miserable Sanchez spread.'

'But you can't,' Millie wailed, 'Luis and his family would lose everything!'

'That's the general idea,' Carter snarled pushing his face up against the girl's. 'Though, o' course, if'n my boy was to get married, I might think about a suitable wedding present. How about it,' the fat man sneered, 'he's allus been sweet on you and if'n he ain't to your taste, well what about his ol'—'

He got no further because an iron hand grasped his collar and jerked him backwards, spilling him on the floor. Before he could speak, a worn broom slapped into his face pushing him back towards the door and a voice he recognized as Reilly's was saying mildly, 'Can't keep this darn place clean, Eustace.

Allus seems like some filth or other's gettin' through the door.'

A final muscular sweep forced Carter on to the wooden sidewalk and the fat man had barely staggered breathlessly to his feet before a skilfully applied boot sped him face downwards into the dust of the street, near where a patiently waiting Pecos had been left, his rein carelessly looped. Pecos needed no tying, he would never willingly leave any vicinity where Fargo Reilly hung his hat.

The little pony turned towards this two-legged victim of his beloved master's wrath and his upper lip drew back over his teeth. Driven half mad by his cavalier treatment, the sight of Reilly's horse apparently laughing at him, drove away the last vestiges of Carter's self-control.

Staggering to his feet, he threw back his quirt-filled right hand preparatory to slashing it across the little mustang's face.

Carter's blow never fell, though, because at the sight of his quirt, Pecos seemed to go mad. The little pony jerked backwards, freeing his rein and, having no room to rear, his head slashed forward, strong yellow teeth closing inches from Carter face as the fat man, seeing his danger, scuttled backwards emitting a pig-like squeal and falling into the street again as he did so.

It might all have ended there, but before the fighting-mad Pecos could trample Carter to jam, Reilly was at his head, speaking softly. Instantly, the little mustang was in hand and allowed his master to lead him back to the rail.

'How much do you want for that two-bit crow bait, goddamit?' a harsh, breathless voice demanded as Reilly, having finished with a now calm, mildly ear-flicking Pecos, turned to go back in the office.

'He ain't for sale, dude,' Reilly answered dispassionately. 'But I'll tell you what I'll do, Fatso,' he went on, 'you can have 'im for nothin' . . . if you can ride 'im for five minutes by the clock.'

A crowd had gathered by this time, with that sort of natural talent Westerners have for sensing trouble, and Carter knew that to decline this two-bit drifter's offer would mean a serious loss of face.

'Sure,' the fat man snapped assuming a confidence he was far from feeling,

'I'll ride that goddam piece o' crow bait and when I own him, I'll shoot the goddam little bastard.'

'First catch your pony.' Reilly responded easily. 'He's there just waiting for you. And your five minutes is runnin'.'

Warily, Carter moved up behind the little mustang but as he reached forward to gather up the reins, Pecos's head jerked round and the big yellow teeth closed with a vicious snap on the place where Carter's hand had been only moments before.

'Goddam it,' the fat man snarled. 'How the hell can I ride the bastard if'n I can't get on him?'

'Cowboys bin askin' that question as long as there's been cows to be punched and horses to be rode,' a whimsical voice, which sounded suspiciously like Long Travis, offered from the crowd.

The ensuing burst of laughter added the final straw. Carter's face mottled and with a vicious snatch, he secured the reins and hurled himself into the saddle in a single movement altogether surprising for one so corpulent.

For a single second, it seemed that even Pecos was taken aback. But if the little animal experienced any surprise in his canny equine brain, it didn't last more than that single second.

Carter had barely thrust his feet into the stirrups of Reilly's worn saddle when the little mustang erupted.

He jerked backwards, away from the hitching rail, rearing and flicking round in seemingly the same movement, so swift was his response.

With a desperate snatch at the saddle horn, Carter managed to remain seated, despite losing a stirrup as he jerked his foot away from a vicious snap at his booted foot.

'Five minutes, huh,' Dusty Rhodes snorted, carefully examining the watch over Reilly's shoulder. 'I'll give anyone two to one in dollars that he don't last one minute!'

'No bet!' his old time friend Long Travis snorted, immediately becoming helpless with laughter as a canny Pecos, sidestepped and almost nonchalantly divested himself of the two-legged nuisance that had tried to usurp his master's place.

Carter left the saddle like a cork from a soda-pop bottle and landed squarely on the hitching rail in front of the *Tribune*'s office, which disintegrated spectacularly under his weight.

Dazed and winded from his unaccustomed exercise, the fat man looked across to where a contented

91

Pecos was nuzzling at the pocket of Reilly's Levis as the lean cowboy rubbed gently at his pony's ears.

Somehow the sight swept away the last vestiges of Carter's reason as, oblivious to consequences, he lumbered to his feet, dragging at the gun concealed under his armpit.

Whether Reilly or his mount was the target of Carter's wrath never became clear, because before his weapon was clear of its holster, the *Tribunes*'s old office broom whammed down on his head, staggering him back into the dust of the street, while Millie Grafton's voice screamed, 'Fargo, look out!'

Before Carter could move or even take his hand from the concealed pistol, he found himself menaced by a dozen guns. With the ease of long practice, Long Travis shifted behind the recumbent ranch boss and swiftly divested him of his weapon, while making sure that Carter had no other surprises concealed about this person.

'You're a rat, Carter,' Reilly gritted, as the big man lumbered heavily to his feet, 'a big fat murdering, thievin' rat with a lot o' money and land you stole from better folks than you. An' I aim to prove what you are to all the folks in this town and way up to the state capital. You ever pull a gun on me again and I'll kill you.'

Abruptly. Reilly swung aboard his mount and headed him towards Grafton's house and corral.

For a long moment Carter stared after his tormentor, then with almost a physical effort he dragged a smile on to his face and turned to the waiting crowd.

'Well, boys,' he began expansively, 'I don't often

lose my wool, but I sure done it pretty well today. Guess that means the drinks are on me!' The fickle crowd cheered him to a man as he led the way into the Long Branch but Dusty Rhodes, only then returning his battered Colts to their worn holsters, didn't fail to notice the venomous look that swept over him and Travis and followed Fargo Reilly down the street.

'By the way,' Grafton offered as, later that day, Reilly bent to begin the, for him, laborious task of setting type for the *Tribune*'s front page, 'did you know that Raoul Sanchez had done a deal with Carter?'

'What sort of deal?' Reilly asked, mildly interested.

'Raoul was sellin' Fatso Mesa de Negro,' came the surprising reply.

'Sellin' . . . but why in hell would he do a stupid thing like that!' Reilly ejaculated and swiftly described the result of his investigations on the Sanchez property.

'Can't say why he'd do it,' Grafton admitted, 'but he was sure set on it. I know,' he went on, forestalling Reilly's question, ' 'cause Leon told me, night afore them skunks raided the bank and shot him.'

'I'll tell you this much, though,' the old man went on. 'If Raoul was set on the idea, it was 'cause he had a damn good reason. That Mex was as smart as a coyote when it came to business.'

'Not the sort then to take out a mortgage on the place if'n he hadn't figgered a way o' makin' good on it afore the note came due?' Reilly mused.

'Hell no,' Grafton confirmed. 'Raoul's pa lost a

good ranch in Mexico to the banks in '57 that way. Raoul was scared stiff of the same thing happenin' here. He wouldn't have nothin' to do with banks, except to cash his cheque for the flock every year.'

CHAPTER ELEVEN

'*Sí*, Fargo, all of what you say is true,' Luis Sanchez said despondently. '*Mí padre*, Don Raoul, would never have anything to do with banks. That is why I cannot understand this paper for fifty thousand dollars.'

'You sure it's your pa's fist?' Reilly demanded, then seeing the youngster's look of incomprehension, explained. 'It's his signature, his *manos*, his hand?'

'Oh, *sí*,' Sanchez responded, 'I would know it. And how could it be otherwise?' he asked simply. 'The paper has only been in Señor Wilson's office. I saw it before that . . . coyote, Carter took over the bank. *Madre de dios, qui . . .*' he lapsed into Spanish and Reilly interrupted hurriedly, knowing the boy was fresh from an interview with the fat rancher turned banker.

'How long's he givin' you, Luis?' Reilly asked, stopping the flow of fluent cursing.

'The note has ten days more to run. Carter says on the morning of the eleventh day, he will sell the ranch at auction. . . .'

'An' I'd bet Pecos and my saddle that the only bid'll be from a certain gent called Lucas Carter,' Reilly said musingly.

'You know your pa'd struck a deal with Carter?' he asked and at the younger man's nod, went on. 'Why'd you figger he decided to sell?'

'I have no idea,' Sanchez shrugged, a look of perplexity replacing the mask of anger.

'For years,' the young man began, 'my father has had . . . I mean he had had, this dream. Dam the Wahoo where it flows across our land, raise the water level and then cut irrigation ditches. You've seen it, Fargo,' he added. 'It's good land and all he needed was the OK from your *amigo*, Señor Corcoran, and the money from the State would have been there. A loan arranged by the governor himself.

'Whether he farmed it himself or leased it to others,' the young man went on, 'we would have made a fortune. It was his dream,' Sanchez finished despairingly. 'So why would he just . . . give it up?'

'Not without a damn good reason,' Reilly mused, after the boy had said his farewells. 'Wonder if it was the same reason that made him try and take a shot at me?'

'What d'you figger, Dusty?' Reilly asked of the squat cowboy, who had sat without speaking during Sanchez's tale of woe.

'I don't,' Rhodes replied laconically, 'it plain don't make no sense. Though me and Travis,' he went on more cheerfully, gesturing at his loquacious partner as the tall one slid into Sanchez's vacated seat, 'have got one piece of good news. We found the Diablos' hideout!'

'Sure it's them,' Reilly demanded, 'not just some sod buster's dugout in the hills?'

'Sure it's them,' Travis snapped abruptly. 'Ol' Billy led us straight there, just like a crow flyin', though in his case,' the lean cowhand corrected himself, 'mebbe I should say, buzzard.'

'We done like you said, Fargo,' Rhodes went on, glaring his partner to silence. 'Watched the Circle C ranch house an' the day after the robbery, sure enough, Kronos heads for the hills on his pet horse. We followed him, easy like, 'til he come on this old line shack.'

'Just an old soddy it was,' Travis interrupted, 'with a corral in back.'

'How many horses?' Reilly asked.

'Six,' Rhodes returned, 'but when Billy rode up, only four *hombres* come out of the cabin to meet him.'

'So, two on look-out duty?' Reilly suggested.

'There are two easy ways in, so that was what we figgered,' Travis answered, dropping his voice abruptly.

'Me and the runt scouted some,' he went on softly, 'and we got the pair of 'em spotted. They both had them red bandannas hung round their necks, Fargo,' Travis finished, 'so we figgered that cinched it.'

'They see either of you while you was playin' "Last of the Mohicans"?' Reilly asked bluntly.

'Son, me and the runt was stealing horses with the Comanche, down on the Pecos, afore you learned to piss straight,' he was quietly informed. 'Ain't no cowhand gonna see me or him, less'n we want 'em to.'

'Sure, nice to know you got some use,' Reilly returned, with a grin. 'You better tell me the way there, if'n you can remember it then, grandpa.' Which, with a lopsided grin at his side partner, Travis proceeded to do. In minute detail.

'Goddam it, Costain, I done tol' you last time there ain't no way anyone's gonna bust this press. It's just too goddam heavy.'

The words dropped crisply into the night-time stillness and Reilly, returning to his room after the usual nightly visit to Pecos, slipped across the side-walk and, avoiding the square of light thrown from the *Tribune*'s window, edged round and carefully pressed his nose up to the glass.

Inside, the office looked like the aftermath of a tornado. Type, paper and ink littered the floor and not content with that, four men were trying to turn the big Gutenberg on its side.

Unfortunately for their plans, a Gutenberg large plate mechanical printing press weighs in at about a ton and a half and it stood, four square on its legs, and laughed at the men's puny efforts.

Finally one of the group, plainly the leader, stood back and swore violently.

'No call for that, Jake,' one of the group instantly retorted. 'Take ye not the Lord's name in vain.'

'Preacher, shet your mouth,' the other snapped, before suddenly finding himself looking down the muzzle of an ancient percussion pistol.

'Brother Jake,' the one referred to as Preacher began, gesturing with the pistol, 'one day you'll go too—' That was as far as he got because suddenly Jake Costain swept the gun aside and drove a crashing blow to the other's jaw.

'We ain't got time for this,' the leader stormed, scratching wildly beneath his red bandanna. 'Get that preachin' bastard on his feet and then pile all the paper agin that press. Hogan,' he finished, addressing one of the four remaining men, 'get that kerosene.'

'Don't waste your time with the paper, boys,' came a mild voice from the doorway, accompanied by an ominous and significant *click*. 'Just shuck your guns and then you can make a start clearin' up the place.'

Making no effort to obey, Costain turned towards the voice, to find Reilly lounging against the door frame, with a cocked Remington pointing at the Diablo leader's favourite belly.

'Take your time, boys,' Reilly suggested, watching narrowly as Costain edged towards the lamp which had been placed on the table.

'Do what he says, boys.' their leader began, shoulders slumping as he turned away from his captor before suddenly leaping towards the table and sweeping the lamp to the floor, but not, however, before Reilly had driven a bullet through the upper part of his arm, knocking him to the floor.

Without waiting to see the result of his shot, Reilly dropped instantly to the floor, avoiding the hail of lead sent his way, and quickly wormed his way through the office door, which he had left open against just such an emergency.

Inside, he could hear Costain groaning, the groan abruptly terminated, as the Diablos' leader suddenly realized that Reilly might have gambled a bullet on the accuracy of his hearing.

Costain was proved right when one of the gang bellowed, 'Jake, where in hell are you—' His words were abruptly terminated as flame lanced from the doorway, the thud of a body issuing a grim warning against anyone wanting to repeat his question.

'Speak up boys,' Reilly suggested, easing himself behind the door frame as he spoke. 'There's plenty o' lead for everybody.'

Grimly, Costain forced himself backwards, freezing in terror at every sound, until smell told him he was next to the one known as Preacher.

'We gotta get outa here, Preacher,' he began in a whisper, feeling the man nod in agreement.

'Get to the back door,' he went on, speaking close to the man's ear, 'when you've got the horses ready, whistle and the rest of us can make a break for it. Get goin',' he finished before the man could object. In a second, Preacher was gone, with barely a creak of the back door, while Costain busied himself with the painful task of trying to get his gun arm into working order.

Suddenly, a shrill whistle split the night and Costain forced himself to his feet, bellowing. 'Get a goin', boys! Preacher's got the horses out back!' There was a rush for the door, with the badly wounded Costain last, every man expecting a bullet at any second.

But no shots were fired, even as the first man wrenched the flimsy door aside and the gang tumbled into the back alley, clawing at the restive horses and swinging aboard.

In seconds, every man was mounted, with the exception of the cursing Costain, when a burst of gunfire erupted from the corner of the *Tribune* building. As one man, the gang turned, leaving their helpless leader, whose mount, spooked by the gunfire, jerked free from its owner and bolted after its companions.

On his knees in the dust, Costain heard once again the hated voice which had presaged all the troubles of the night.

'Best get on your feet, Jake,' Reilly suggested mildly, slipping away his freshly reloaded pistol. 'Sounds like the marshal's comin' and I'd bet a stack he's got a nice warm cell all picked out for you.' A shout from behind the cover supplied by Reilly's recently vacated corner of the *Tribune* building apprised Reilly of the presence of Defoe and after calling to him the all clear, Reilly turned back to the still bleeding and monotonously cursing bandit leader.

'Now don't you take on so, Jake, your shoulder don't look so bad,' Reilly offered sympathetically. 'I'd give, oh, mebbe, three to one, that you'll live to hang.'

'You ain't got nothing on me!' Costain sneered, but the fear was plain in the man's bloodshot eyes.

'Leader of the Diablos killed the banker,' Reilly explained simply, flicking at the red bandanna around his prisoner's neck. 'You're the leader, so it must have been you. Description fits, too,' he pointed out, before adding, 'unless, o'course, you ain't the leader. But if'n you ain't, you sure better be ready with a name when the marshal asks you. I ain't sure,' Reilly finished shrewdly, 'but I don't guess Billy Kronos'd be so ready to swing in your place.'

'I don't know who you mean,' Costain returned shakily, as Bud Defoe and Will Sovereign jerked the man unsympathetically to his feet.

'Sure you don't,' Defoe nodded gently. 'You finished here, Fargo?' he asked with a wink, and after receiving Reilly's nod, jerked his head towards the jail.

'Help me with him, Will,' Reilly heard Defoe begin as the group walked away. 'And in the morning, see the Chinaman and tell him we're gonna need us a scaffold and a lot o' rope. This one's got a thick neck, so . . .' the rest of the gruesome details were lost in the darkness and Reilly grinned.

'I don't know about ol' Jake,' he admitted to the darkness, 'but Bud's sure scarin' the hell outa me!'

Early morning sunshine had barely chased night-time shadows from its roof-tops, when a dainty, well set-up bay gelding turned into the main street of Verdad de Soleil.

The horse paced slowly, its rider obviously checking the buildings, until, when opposite Carter's Long Branch saloon, the gelding was halted with an unnecessarily savage jerk, before being directed to the hitching rail.

Its rider, a small slim man well below average height, secured his mount to the post and pausing only to loosen his pearl-handled, silver-mounted Colts in their fancy fast-draw holsters, he turned abruptly and made his way to the door at the rear of the saloon.

A single tap sufficed to gain him admittance and he was shown, with a deference amounting to terror, into the well appointed office on the second floor.

Arrogantly, the little man selected a cigar from the humidor on the desk and settled himself in Carter's comfortable chair behind the big desk.

'I see you're makin' yourself at home,' Carter's voice said from the doorway as the fat man hove into view, belting a garish dressing-gown around his corpulent belly as he did so.

'Ain't bad for a hog wallow,' the little man returned easily. 'How you bin, Lucas?'

'Fair to middlin', Lane,' the big man admitted, sliding into a seat opposite his guest and selecting a cigar himself.

With the cigar going to his satisfaction, Carter began affably, 'Got a little job for you, Lane. Fella round town gettin' too nosey to suit me. Want you to deal with him. How does five thousand sound?'

'Sounds real sweet,' the little gunman admitted. 'My own mother wouldn't be worth keepin' alive for that kinda money,' and the two men grinned at each other in savage understanding.

CHAPTER TWELVE

'I don't care how you get to him, you little bastard,' Jake Costain hissed, in a savage whisper, 'just tell Kronos I better be outa here before the circuit judge arrives or . . . he'll know or what, I guess!'

It was noon of the day Lane Walker had ridden into town and Carter had sent Ansel Raikes with a message of reassurance to the imprisoned Costain. It turned out that reassurance was the last thing Costain was looking for,

'Don't forget,' Costain snarled, as a frightened Raikes backed away from the cell. 'You tell 'im, now.'

'You figger it's sensible lettin' Ansel scurry back and forwards with his li'l messages? An' how in hell'd you know Ansel was workin' for Carter?' Defoe demanded, as Reilly eased his chair forward from its place by the doorway leading from the front of the marshal's office, where both were sitting, into the rear of the building occupied by the cells. Abruptly, both heard the bang of the rear door closing.

'Why not?' asked Reilly, who had overheard all Costain had had to say. 'He ain't good enough with a

104

gun to do any harm,' the cowboy continued, 'even if
one of us was stupid enough to let him get the drop.
And don't forget, we only need to let him tell Carter
what we want him to know.

'An' the answer to your second question is, only
Ansel could've left the back door open when the
Circle C boys whomped Will on the head and tried to
lynch Luis,' Reilly finished.

'Sure, but still . . .' Defoe began slowly, only to stop
as the office door banged back on its hinges, to admit
a breathless Will Sovereign.

'Bud,' the lean deputy began without preamble,
'Lane Walker's back in town. He's drinking with
Carter in the Long Branch, and I just seen Luis
Sanchez headin' that way.'

'I never could stand the stink o' greasers,' the flat,
surprisingly deep voice began. 'It allus reminds me of
a pig farm.'

Luis Sanchez turned from the bar to glance in the
direction of the speaker. He saw a short, slim individual, dressed in fancy cowboy style, standing
between him and the crudely carved batwing doors,
and wearing a pair of pearl-handled guns as though
he knew how to use them. The little man turned,
thereby placing his back to the opening, and spoke
again, plainly addressing Sanchez.

'If'n you wanta go on breathin', you dirty thievin'
greaser bastard, you better get down on your knees
and crawl outa here. Do that,' the little gunman went
on, almost reasonably, 'I may let you live . . . this time.'

Abruptly the killer's hands twitched as Sanchez

put his drink carefully on the bar and turned to face his own certain death. He opened his mouth to speak, but the voice, when it came, was from entirely another direction.

'Walker, shuck that belt, pronto. And you, Luis, get out now!'

Making no move to obey, Walker placed his hands on his hips. 'And if I don't—?' he began, only to be interrupted by the blast from a shotgun, which tore up a foot-long section of the polished bar and showered him with splinters.

Enraged at the destruction of his property, Carter began to rise from his place at the main card table, only to freeze into immobility as a cold voice said from the shadows of his own back stairs, 'Easy all! Mr Carter, you better think again.

'It's good advice, Carter,' Bud Defoe reiterated, motioning to the Circle C contingent as a relieved Luis Sanchez moved quickly past him and a white-faced Lane Walker began to reach for his belt. 'You be real careful how you get rid o' that belt, Walker,' the old peace officer snarled.

The fancy belt thudded to the floor.

'Get over with the rest o' the scum, Walker,' Defoe snapped, moving sideways to cover the group and prevent Walker coming between him and the other men who, at an abrupt jerk of the shotgun's barrels, hurriedly began to divest themselves of weapons.

'I'd have thought you'd need better help than a man who lets hisself get buffaloed and his prisoner taken,' Carter sneered, leaning back as the last Colt dropped to the floor.

'Oh, Will's a good man,' Defoe returned mildly, never moving his eyes or shotgun from Walker's' face. 'He just ain't got eyes in the back of his head is all and when some coward and liar sneaks up behind a feller, well, ain't much even a good man can do.'

'Are you meanin' me, you old fool . . .' Kronos began, jerking upright.

'Pick up that gun, Billy,' Bud Defoe interrupted mildly. 'Go ahead, fill your hand. But if'n you do, I'm just naturally gonna cut you in half and call it self-defence. Just give me an excuse, Billy . . . please!' The last word was a vicious hiss and a white-faced and badly frightened Billy Kronos sank quickly back into his chair.

Without another glance in his direction, the old marshal said, 'You remember what I'm gonna tell you now, Walker,' he began, glaring down at the little gunman. 'Self-defence won't work for a gunny like you. You use them Colts on anyone in this town and I'll hang you, within the hour. And that's a promise. And it holds for any other border trash you bring in, Carter,' Defoe added, looking past the killer at his corpulent employer.

Without easing the hammer of his weapon, Defoe transferred the barrels to the crook of his left arm and backed to the doors of the saloon, before moving smoothly through them into the welcoming sunlight.

'Goddam that old—' Walker began hysterically, rising from his chair and scooping up his belt.

'Whatever you was gonna say,' Carter interrupted, 'it's a waste of breath. That old man knows too much,' he went on thoughtfully, glancing across at Kronos. 'I think he'll just naturally have to go.'

'Just say the word,' the heavy-set foreman snarled. 'Just tell me when!'

'Sure,' Carter nodded agreement, 'but mebbe not just yet.'

'You handled it real sweet, considering,' Fargo Reilly informed Defoe as he eased the hammer of his heavy calibre Winchester and fell in beside the older man as they backed across the street, so as still to face the doors of the Long Branch, pausing only to allow a hurrying Will Sovereign to join them from the back of the saloon.

'Yeah,' Defoe growled, 'only thing is, after he thinks for a while, Carter'll probably realize that I can't be everywhere at once. Oh, Walker won't try nothin' too raw but that ain't gonna save young Luis . . . or you,' he finished, watching Reilly's face.

'You sure called that right, Bud,' Will Sovereign agreed. 'What d'you figger to do, Fargo?'

'Easy,' the lean cowboy shrugged, 'you're headin' for Black Mesa and you're gonna tell Sanchez to stay put 'til he hears from me. Tell ol' Diego, too, in case that boy ain't hearin' so good.'

'OK,' Defoe responded, 'that takes care of Sanchez. What about you?'

'Oh, I'm headin for the hills,' Reilly answered and was gone, on his way to collect Pecos, before either of the bewildered peace officers could think of a suitable retort.

*

'Headin' down stream,' Reilly grunted, rising to his feet and reaching for Pecos's trailing rein. 'Nothing we can do but follow 'em, I guess.'

It was morning of the day after Reilly's departure from town and Pecos and his master had quickly located the mule tracks that seemed so significant when Reilly had last seen them.

'This is real interestin',' the cowboy offered. 'Sometimes the tracks o' that big stud of Sanchez's is over Corcoran's mule and his horse and sometimes it's the other way round.

'Which means, before you tell me same,' Reilly went on as Pecos nodded his head wisely, 'that the two of them was probably ridin' together.'

Suddenly, Reilly pulled his mount to a halt and stared intently at a large patch of dried mud some little way off the main trail. Several clear hoofprints were baked into the clay, the big ones belonging to Sanchez's stallion, those of the mule Corcoran had been using for his gear and the smaller prints of the horse the government man had been riding. The prints were clear and easily recognizable, just like the trail Reilly had been so scrupulously following for the past hour. Except they were going back down the mountain. And something about the tracks of Corcoran's animal had Reilly swinging out of the saddle.

'Just like the others,' he muttered to himself, 'except. . . .'

For several minutes, Reilly studied the inoffensive patch of mud from all angles, then he stood up with a confirmatory grunt.

'Just like the others,' he told himself, 'except on the way down, Corcoran's pony weren't carrying no weight.'

Some two hundred yards away from the rough, rock strewn trail that Reilly was following, Karl Straker was an interested spectator to these proceedings. His pony having pulled up lame, Straker had been leading the animal back to the home ranch, not, it should be noted, because of any concern for his mount's welfare, but because Lucas Carter took a very dim view of any avoidable damage to something that was his property, even a forty-dollar cow pony.

Straker had stopped amongst the pine to rest just as Reilly had turned the corner of the trail and with the wind blowing from Pecos to the Circle C man, the little pony had given Reilly no warning of the other's presence.

Having completed his examination of that part of the trail, Reilly swung into the saddle and, not wishing to lose sight of him, Straker mounted and kicked his unwilling pony into a fast walk after him.

The trail Reilly was following came to an abrupt halt, some distance from the edge of the cliffs which constituted the bank of the Wahoo at this point. Clearly, all three animals had been tied to the single scraggy pine tree, which clung to existence in the poor soil, but between that and the edge of the cliff, the ground was covered with the flat, everlasting scree, which made walking difficult for a pony and showed no tracks whatsoever.

With a shrug Reilly swung down, secured Pecos to the stunted pine and advanced carefully to the edge of the cliff. He looked down, noting the surge and push of the current as it raced between the rock walls and observing also that, only a couple of yards from where he stood, a narrow, treacherous path appeared to descend the cliff-face, leading to a minute ledge directly below him, which disappeared around an overhanging spur of rock.

Perplexed by this surprising turn of events, Reilly shoved his battered Stetson to the back of his head and turned back towards Pecos, just as a shot rang out from the pines above him.

Over the sights of his Sharps, Straker watched exultantly as Reilly pitched backwards and disappeared into the ravine of the Wahoo.

'And I'm guessin' that's the finish of you, Mr Busy Body,' the Circle C man grunted, as he dropped another enormous cartridge into the breech of his rifle and jerked up the loading lever.

With his weapon reloaded, the killer moved out of the cover of the pine forest and made his way to the edge of the cliff.

Carefully, Straker leaned over the almost sheer drop and what he saw brought a grunt of satisfaction.

Of Reilly, there was no sign but in the far distance, floating lightly on the foaming water, Straker could just determine a battered Stetson, which he recognized at once as his victim's property.

'Looks like I was right,' he told himself. 'And weren't it lucky for me that I just happened to come on this nice little ridin' horse, whose owner don't look like he'll have no more use for it?'

Pecos, however, had other ideas. He was Reilly's

horse and no two-legged nuisance was going to get a leg over his saddle.

After several abortive attempts to snatch up the little pony's reins, the last of which nearly cost Straker his trigger finger, the Circle C man swore violently and swung aboard his own badly limping pony.

'I guess you'll be a little more pleased to see me after a couple of days with no food or grub,' he informed a grinning Pecos.

Jerking his pony's head around, Straker spurred him towards the Circle C, confident that now after hearing his news, Carter would begin to treat him with the respect he deserved.

CHAPTER THIRTEEN

Evening had fallen over Verdad de Soleil and in the jail, Will Sovereign was settling down to his share of the night shift, while in the back room of Miguel Ortez's little cantina, Mrs Ortez sighed unhappily as she realized that a night-time vigil of another sort would, for her, soon be over.

Leon Wilson was as white as the sheet upon which he lay. Occasionally, he lapsed into mumbling incoherence, but most of the time he simply lay, body wracked at intervals by the spasmodic cramps which were the only outward signs of the fever consuming him.

Sonya Ortez looked down at the thin, wasted form she had nursed steadfastly for the past days. True, he was a gringo, but as she had told her husband, with her own brand of simple logic, the first and only time he had ever remonstrated with her over taking in a wounded man. 'How can I leave him to die in the street?' and Miguel Ortez, realizing the quality of the girl he had married, had simply smiled and motioned Luca Inez, his handy man, to take the man's legs.

That had been many years before today and now Sonya Ortez sat, as she had before, waiting for a man to die.

Without warning, Wilson's eyes flickered open and for the first time in days, the fevered light was gone from them. Wearily, his mouth opened as, to save him pain and trouble, Sonya bent forward, listening carefully.

A minute later, she was out of the room and calling her husband.

'Miguel, Miguel! Señor Wilson is awake and . . . and he wants to talk to the sheriff.'

'Looks to me like he's gone,' Defoe offered as he stood back from the bed but Sonya Ortez gave a knowing head-shake, placing a gentle hand on her patients' chest.

'No,' she said firmly, 'he is still alive but for how much longer, *quien sabe?*'

'What did he say, Señor Bud?' Ortez asked quietly.

'He said the mortgage on Luis Sanchez place was a forgery,' Defoe stated, 'but he passed out before he could tell me who done it.'

'I'm guessin',' Defoe explained to Sovereign, as the two peace officers took their ease in the jail sometime later, 'that Wilson did the pen work but Carter was blackmailin' him into it.'

'That'd sure make sense,' Sovereign admitted, 'seein' how it was Carter got all the benefit.

'Thing is, though, Bud, how you gonna play it?' Sovereign went on earnestly. 'You only got the word

114

of a dyin' man against one of the biggest men in the territory.'

'What I'm figgerin' to do,' Defoe began maliciously, 'is let the fat bastard have enough rope to hang hisself. . . .'

And while Defoe explained his plans in detail to his deputy, Jake Costain, listening by the rear door, which Sovereign had inadvertently left open, heard each and every word.

'I gotta get outa here,' Costain hissed at Ansel Raikes as the other came with his food later that evening, leaving Sovereign alone in the outer office.

'Sure, Jake,' Raikes began placatingly, 'the boss is working on it right now, according to Billy. You just sit tight and—'

'Goddam it. We ain't got time for that!' Costain snapped, 'the whole mess of us are in bad trouble and I gotta tell the boss about it.'

'Come here,' Costain motioned to the unsuspecting Raikes, 'an' see what you think. . . .' But as the scrawny jailor came within reach, Costain lunged.

One brawny hand grasped Raikes's greasy collar and before he could react, Costain had rapidly divested him of the keys to the cell and a battered Remington from the holster under his arm.

It was the work of barely a moment to open the cell door and then Costain was ushering the unwilling Raikes towards the opening.

' No . . . no . . .' the scrawny jailor drew back on the very threshold of the cell. 'I ain't stayin', for God's sake,' Raikes whined. 'The sheriff won't never believe I weren't in on it. You gotta take me with you!'

For a moment Costain hesitated, fingering the Remington, then abruptly he jerked his head and, with Raikes following, both men slipped through the partially open back door, leaving Will Sovereign the sole occupant of the jail.

The pair had gone only a few hundred yards, when Raikes grabbed Costain's arm and pulled his companion to a halt.

'What is this,' the scrawny jailer began. 'Where are we goin'—?' He was interrupted by the dull roar of the heavy Remington breaking across the evening stillness and, without a sound, Raikes slumped bonelessly to the floor.

'I don't know where you might be heading,' Costain said callously, giving the body a kick as he carefully ejected the spent cartridge from Raikes's battered revolver and snapped the loading gate closed, 'but once they find that case, with that goddam Reilly missing, you may just be more use to us dead than you ever was alive.'

'That was good work, Costain,' Carter complimented after the Diablos' leader had described his activities, having arrived at the fat man's second floor office by way of the Long Branch's back door.

'I'm figgerin' it leaves us holdin' all the aces. And with Lane here as our new marshal, we can't lose,' the fat man finished, slapping the little gunman on the back.

'Ain't you forgettin' about something?' Walker demanded truculently. 'Town's already got a marshal, last time I looked.'

116

'I don't forget nothin',' Carter snapped, 'and you might do well to remember that. No,' he added thoughtfully, glancing across at the Circle C fore-man, 'I have a feelin' that Marshal Defoe is gonna be, eh . . . retired in the very near future. But I don't imagine that'll cause anyone too much grief!'

'No grief at all,' Billy Kronos sneered, joining in the general laughter.

First of all, there was pain, a flaring, burning pain that seemed to grow out of a great dark pit of suffer-ing, behind eyelids that required too great an act of will to force open.

And finally, when he did manage to force his eyelids back, Reilly immediately wished he hadn't.

Early morning sunlight was slanting down on him as he lay on the narrow trail he had previously seen from above, behind a wide, flat spur of rock that, by unaccountable good luck, had concealed him from Straker.

'Sure wish this head belonged to someone else,' Reilly told himself as he slowly managed to force himself into a sitting position, massaging the overnight stiffness from his limbs and apparently paying no attention to the mouth of the low cave a bare yard away.

He closed his eyes again, letting the dizziness wash away, only to jerk upright as he recalled the circum-stances of his fall. Automatically, Reilly eased the old Remington from its holster and began carefully to make his way up the narrow path to the top of the cliff.

The last part was only managed by a desperate scramble, but eventually he crouched, winded but otherwise unhurt, behind a convenient boulder.

Pecos still stood by the pine tree, patiently awaiting the coming of his master and reassured by his equine companion's demeanour, Reilly stood up and slipped away his pistol.

'No one around, huh?' he demanded, rubbing at the velvety muzzle. 'You sure called it wrong last time, though, didn't you? Now we got to get to work.'

A rope snaked down the cliff face made short work of the difficult pathway and, having left Pecos to a scanty meal of oats and the last of his water, it wasn't long before Reilly stood again in front of the low cave he had noted on his last visit.

'Better make this quick,' he grunted, counting his few matches, 'looks like we ain't gonna have light for long.'

As it turned out, he needn't have worried because upon entering the low cave, he found that a narrow chimney at the rear combined with light from the front gave all the illumination he needed. More than he needed in reality, because the first thing he saw in the light from the entrance was the dead and partially mummified countenance of Hymie Corcoran.

'Don't look like he took much killin',' Reilly mumbled to himself. 'Back o' the skull's hardly got a dent in it.'

Finishing his cursory physical examination, Reilly swiftly went through the corpse's pockets. Nothing unusual came to light, until he gingerly delved into the inside pocket of Corcoran's mouldy suit, where he found a sheaf of neatly folded papers.

Carefully, Reilly drew them out and began to read, but he was barely half-way through the first page when he stopped and turned back to the beginning. Ten minutes later, he was finished and standing up to push the crumbling papers carefully into a pocket of his worn vest.

Leaving the cave, he ascended his rope and swung quickly aboard the waiting Pecos. His expression was grim because he knew now the reason behind Raoul Sanchez's attempt on his life and why the Mexican sheep man had abandoned his life-long dream of turning the Black Mesa into an agricultural paradise.

'I just hope I can pull young Luis out from under,' he informed the little mustang as he turned Pecos towards town and encouraged him into a gallop.

Another day of heat and dust was shifting imperceptibly into the cool of evening as Marshal Bud Defoe stepped off the porch of his office cum jail and trudged across the street to the hotel and his evening meal.

Will Sovereign remained in the office in charge of the jail and Ansel Raikes's corpse, kept in a spare cell until Lee, the undertaker, could attend to it.

Behind the marshal, two noiseless shadows detached themselves from the wall of a nearby building where they had been patiently waiting and fell in on either side of him.

As Defoe reached the shadows of the hotel building, the man in the lead put a hand to his belt, reaching up as he did to grab the marshal's arm. Before he could touch his victim, however, Reilly's voice said from the shadows behind him, '*Saludos*, nice night for a murder, huh?'

CHAPTER
FOURTEEN

Give him his due, the back-up man was fast. The words had barely left Reilly's mouth before the second man had twisted, his knife-hand flashing back for the throw.

Not quite quick enough, though, because before his hand could start its forward motion, Reilly's first shot tore into his chest throwing him back against his companion and causing the latter's knife merely to cut a sliver out of the flesh over Bud Defoe's rib cage, instead of puncturing the lung as his attacker intended.

Before he could recover his balance, the butt of Defoe's ever ready shotgun crashed into the side of his skull, removing any interest he might have had in subsequent events.

'Christ, Fargo, you sure pick your moments, don't you? Couldn't have left it any later, I guess?' Defoe demanded, beginning to shake with reaction.

'Could've done,' Reilly admitted, looking up from his examination of the body. 'Your price is sure goin' up though,' he offered, displaying the two gold pieces he had removed from the pocket of his first victim.

'Ansel's dead,' Defoe began as Reilly helped him carry the surviving assassin back to the office.

'Figgers.' Reilly said, having heard Defoe's account of Wilson's story. 'And that explains why Carter tried to get to you. They gotta get rid of all the witnesses. Get a bucket o' water, Will,' he went on, addressing Sovereign, I'm figgerin' we better wake this *hombre* up.'

But Defoe's attacker was still unconscious when, moments later, there was a fusillade of shots from the direction of the *Tribune*'s office.

Reilly was instantly in the street, only to see a bunched group of riders tear out of the alley-way by Grafton's newspaper and gallop up the street. Defoe, next to him, raised his shotgun but before he could fire, Reilly knocked up the barrels.

'They've got Millie – and Connie was with her,' he said bitterly as Defoe looked at him questioningly. 'And I must be awful dumb not to have realized that was Carter's next move.'

Eustace Grafton was dying. Reilly and Defoe found the old newspaper man where he had fallen, trying to defend his granddaughter and Connie, with the rusty old shotgun he had used in his last fight lying under him.

Gently, his old friend Defoe turned him over but one look was enough for both men. They had seen death before.

'Don't look so . . . good . . . this . . . time.' Grafton managed to gasp, opening his eyes with an effort.

'Hell, you'll be fine,' Defoe lied manfully. 'Have you up and around in no time, you ol' buzzard.'

'Liar,' Grafton said, without heat. 'Afore I cash . . . in,' he went on desperately, 'letter from . . . Wilson . . . my . . . desk. About . . . Carter . . . I think.'

Suddenly pain wracked the old man's frame and his hand shot out, grasping Reilly's arm. Grafton's face was livid and his eyes glazing as he said, 'Fargo . . . Carter . . . got Millie – and Connie, too . . . she . . . visiting. . . . Get them boy . . . and kill all those . . . bast—' But this last effort was too much and Grafton jerked once and was still.

For a long second, Reilly remained staring at what was left of the old man who had been his friend. Then he jerked upwards, back off his knees to stand upright.

'You got my word, old man,' he said softly. 'I'll see them all swing for this.'

'Find that letter,' was all Reilly said to Defoe as he turned towards the Ortez cantina. 'Then get Dusty and Long. I've gotta get my gear.'

Ten minutes later, Reilly was back in the marshal's office. On his shirt was the tarnished silver star of a deputy federal marshal and around his waist was the worn fast-draw belt holding his twin Colts. From somewhere he'd also found a battered Stetson.

'Did you find the letter?' Reilly demanded.

'Sure,' Defoe admitted, 'but it's kinda awkward, 'cause it says "Only to be opened in the event of my death". The signature's Wilson's; I recognized it and he ain't dead yet. I've got it locked in my desk.'

'OK,' Reilly acknowledged,' leave that for now.'

'Look,' he went on swiftly, indicating the star on his worn vest, 'this must be kind of a shock but I ain't got time to argue or explain, Bud, and I'm admittin' I need your help,' he finished bluntly.

'That badge goes with me,' Defoe assured him and with a nod, Reilly turned to a dubious looking Dusty Rhodes.

'I know about that little corral you boys have got tucked away in the hills behind Black Mesa,' he stated flatly. 'And I'm here to say you can rob Carter blind for all I care,' he went on as Long and Dusty exchanged worried looks. 'But I want you boys to sign on as deputies for the duration so that if you have to shoot anyone you can do it legal.'

'I ain't sure,' Long began, 'seeing how it might affect our social standing—'

'Shut up!' Rhodes snapped at his old time friend, 'for once just shut up and put up your hand.'

Swiftly, Defoe administered the oath and as a still dubious Long Travis pinned on his badge, he asked, 'What now?'

'Get me a good horse,' Reilly answered, 'grub and cartridges. . . .' but he was talking to himself, Long Travis and Dusty Rhodes were already gone to set about work they understood thoroughly.

'Surely, there ain't no point us riding now, in the dark and all . . . we can't track the bastards.' Defoe began reasonably.

'We don't need to track them,' he was tersely informed. 'When you go skunk killing, best thing to do is go straight to the nest. Let's look at where you found Ansel. Then I gotta send a telegram.'

'You got to admit, Costain thought pretty quick,' Reilly admitted, rising to his feet and tendering the Remington cartridge he had located after a brief search by the flaring light of the torch in Defoe's hand.

'Leaving the cartridge for the new marshal to find "accidentally" was a neat touch,' he went on. 'If'n they'd got you, who would have looked any further?

'With me strung up and his sister prisoner, Sanchez has to sell and Carter scoops the pot. Wonder what that tricky bastard's figgerin' now?' he finished as he led the way towards their waiting ponies.

'Goddam it,' Carter snarled. 'There was two of them greaser bastards! How could they miss one fat ol' man?'

'Reilly horned in,' Lane Walker said simply. 'I gotta feelin' you're gonna have to deal with that fella and do it right quick.'

'I thought I had,' Carter responded, glaring at the room's other occupant, a shocked Karl Straker.

'Didn't you tell me Reilly went into the ravine of the Wahoo?' Carter demanded.

'Boss,' Straker began, lying desperately,' I saw him go in myself—'

'You're a liar,' Carter snapped dispassionately. 'But it don't matter, 'cause Mr Smartass Reilly is gonna be taken care of,' and when Walker looked at him questioningly, the fat man said simply, 'it's done. How don't concern you.'

'All right,' Walker returned, 'but what about the marshal? He's still got enough to finish all of us.'

'Sure,' Carter responded broodingly. 'Hey, Straker,' he snapped abruptly, addressing his discomfited employee, 'how much do you like the marshal?'

'Not much,' responded the rifle expert. 'Why?'

'You figure you'd mebbe like five thousand dollars better?' Carter asked maliciously.

'Whole lot better,' Straker responded, rising and putting on his hat. 'Get your bill fold ready. Defoe's as good as dead.'

At first, fear of her captors' intentions had kept Millie Grafton quiet. But as the night wore on and the red-masked band showed no sign of halting, she had moved her pony up next to Connie Sanchez and the two girls had managed to converse in low whispers.

Their speculations, at least about their destination, were ended a little after dawn, when they topped a shallow rise and found themselves looking down at a spacious cabin, built of unsquared logs, with a hay barn and a corral big enough for about thirty horses standing between the two buildings.

Halting their mounts next to the corral, the kidnappers dragged the two girls from their ponies and after stripping off the riding gear turned the little animals loose, while the girls, their hands still securely tied behind them, were roughly ushered into the house.

The leader of the gang held open the door of what

was plainly the communal bedroom and with a laugh at the girls' expressions growled, 'It sure ain't the Texas House in Dodge, but I'm afraid you . . . ladies are just gonna have to rough it for a while.' With a coarse laugh, he swung the door shut and Millie heard the sound of a heavy bar dropped into place.

Desperately, Millie scanned their prison but without help from the outside, escape for the two girls seemed impossible. True, the single window was only covered by a soiled piece of greased paper, a common enough procedure in the Territory and beyond where glass was expensive and hard to get. But, through the paper, the girls could see the shadow of the thick wooden bars which were nailed across the opening.

'What can they want?' Connie Sanchez demanded, of no one in particular, sitting down and trying to work the ropes binding her wrists into a more comfortable position.

'I guess we'll find out soon enough,' her friend responded.

As it turned out, the girls did not have long to wait. Barely five minutes had passed, when the door of their prison was thrown open to reveal the lean figure and whiskey-bloated face of Rafe Carter.

Without waiting for an invitation, Carter stumbled into the room, bringing with him an odour of week-old sweat and cheap liquor.

Lurching to a halt, he swept off his hat with the hand not occupied by a whiskey bottle and slurred, 'Ladies, I trust your accommo . . . accommod . . . this here bedroom suits you. Kinda tough if'n it don', 'cause we ain't got another one.' He finished, grinning lewdly at his own joke.

'Just why have we been brought here?' Millie demanded, with a confidence she was far from feeling.

'Well,' Carter began, 'that sure depends on you. See, with your Grandpa dead,' he went on brutally, 'that makes you owner of the *Tribune*. Now, my Pa thinks he needs that paper, or at least,' Rafe went on shrewdly, 'he needs someone friendly runnin' it. Ol' man Grafton was stirring' up a hornets' nest for us and Pa wants things quieted down some. So, you're gonna sell to us.'

'And if I don't?' Millie hissed.

'Figure it out for yourself,' Carter snapped, suddenly unaccountably nettled. 'Kidnapped by a bunch of border scourin's. What d'you figger's gonna happen? Come nightfall . . .' he finished lasciviously.

'You wouldn't dare!' Connie Sanchez flared. 'You filthy gringo! When my brother finds you and I tell him what you threatened to do, he'll hang you and his *vaqueros* will quirt the skin off you while you're chokin' your rotten life away!'

'Is that so, Miss High and Mighty!' Carter screamed, dashing the liquor bottle aside and jumping for the still-bound girl. 'In about four days' time, your brother ain't gonna have no *vaqueros* nor no ranch either, 'cause Pa's gonna collect on the mortgage he fixed.'

Lust flamed in Carter's eyes as he forced the slim Mexican girl back towards the bunks that lined the room.

'We was gonna keep you, to bargain with,' her attacker informed her, 'in case that fool of a brother of yours cut up rough but, personally,' he went on, forcing his grimy, bewhiskered face against the girl's pale cheek, while reaching down a hand to open his trousers, 'I don't see why you and me shouldn't have ourselves a little fun right here and now.'

CHAPTER FIFTEEN

But Connie Sanchez came from a race of fighters and she didn't need her hands free to do damage.

Even as Carter turned his head, fumbling for his belt, he brought his ear into close proximity with the girl's strong white teeth and Connie didn't waste her opportunity. Clamping her teeth hard on the sensitive lobe, she jerked backwards, eliciting a scream of agony from Rafe Carter as he tore himself away from her and clamped a hand to his mutilated ear.

Costain appeared instantly in the doorway, a long-barrelled Colt ready in his fist and he stepped quickly between Carter and the girl as – with the pain subsiding – Carter lurched forward to take his revenge.

'Leave her alone,' Costain said, pushing Carter easily away. 'You know what we agreed. Don't start lettin' what's between your legs do your thinkin' for you,' he ordered coarsely. 'When the time comes, we'll all have a turn at the li'l *muchacha*. 'Til then, no one touches her. We may still need her. And them, in case you ain't sure, is your pa's orders.'

Still grumbling and cursing his damaged ear, Rafe

Carter allowed himself to be ushered into the main room of the cabin and, after a while, the girls could hear from the noise that their captors had settled down to a night of whiskey-fuelled carousing.

Connie turned huge eyes, now clearly dilating as the shock hit her, upon her companion.

'I thought he was—'

'You were right,' Millie interrupted briskly, as with a final yank, she freed herself of her bonds and came to sit by her friend.

'We ain't got time for hysterics now, Connie dear,' Millie began, seeing her friend's mouth start to open as the tears began to well. 'Just let me get these ropes off and you'll feel a whole lot better.'

'Best keep them ropes handy,' Millie offered, as, some moments later, she freed the last knot. 'No tellin' what they'll do if they find we've slipped 'em.' Connie nodded obediently, before reaching into her boot to draw out a slim, wicked looking stiletto.

'At least, now if the gentle Señor Carter comes back, I can give him something to remember me by,' she said softly.

'If he comes,' Millie offered callously, 'finish him as quiet as you can. It may give us a chance to get out.'

But it wasn't Carter that provided the night-time distraction. The moon said three o'clock, when Millie was awakened by a soft voice hissing urgently at the window.

'Miz Millie, ma'am, are you in there?'

'Sure,' the girl answered. 'Who's there?'

'It's us, ma'am,' another voice replied. 'Goddamit, Long, keep them ponies quiet. Dusty Rhodes, ma'am,' the voice went on, 'Fargo sent us to say, we're plannin on gettin' you out in the mornin' but—'

A hiss from his companion interrupted the little horse breaker and when Millie looked again there was nothin to be seen or heard. Until, that is one of her kidnappers pushed noisily through the cabin's ill-fitting door and, appearing round the end of the building, began to relieve himself on a stunted cactus growing by the back porch.

Finished at last the man staggered back inside, scratching drowsily, and almost instantly Rhodes was back at the window.

'Ma'am,' he began urgently, 'we can't pull these bars and get you outa there in time for it to be safe 'cause it'll make too much noise. So Fargo's stagin' what you might call a kinda . . . diversion. You be ready to move any time after sun-up, 'cause when we go, we're gonna go right quick. Don't you worry none, the little man finished, 'we're sure gonna get you outa there.'

'I don't like it,' Defoe stated. 'You're just gonna get your fool head blowed off. One man against six. You ain't gotta chance.'

'That's what I'm figgerin' Kronos and his boys'll think,' Reilly responded, as he tightened his saddle's girth in the pre-dawn stillness. 'So then they'll ease up and mebbe get careless.'

'Sure worried about this li'l pony, though,' Reilly went on seriously. 'I'm hopin' he don't stop a slug.'

'Oh, don't you worry none about that there pony,' Defoe snarled, clearly incensed and not a little frightened. 'You'll be the one stoppin' the slugs.'

'Well, good,' Reilly said mildly, 'Long'll probably charge me if'n anything happens to that horse.'

'Dusty, you about set?' Reilly demanded, before an apoplectic Bud Defoe had managed to render himself capable of speech.

'Sure,' came the laconic reply.

'You and Long get agoin' then,' Reilly ordered. 'I'll see you at the cabin and, Long,' he added unnecessarily, 'for Christ's sake, don't forget them signals.'

Manuel Pablo Gonsalez, Pablo to his friends of whom he had few, was not prone to disbelieving his eyes. Not at least, until the second bottle of mescal had done its work.

And this morning he could have sworn he was stone-cold sober. But still, for some reason, the gringo Reilly appeared to be committing suicide by the simple expedient of riding up to the door of the Diablos' hideout as casually as though he were going to town for a drink.

Pablo had begun to doubt the accuracy of his optics, until that is, the apparition pulled its mount to a halt and snapped, 'Get your boss out here and the rest of his scum, pronto. I've come for them girls.'

By the time Pablo was back, followed by Kronos, Costain and three other white men, Reilly was sitting across his saddle, legs dangling down in front of him by his left stirrup.

Silently. Reilly cursed. Where in hell was Rafe Carter?

'You gotta be crazy,' Kronos began, breaking into Reilly's train of thought. 'We're just gonna kill you and keep them girls. But, you know that, don't you?' Kronos went on, watching uneasily as Reilly shifted in the saddle.

Suddenly, from the rear of the building, there came a piercing cowboy yell. Involuntarily, every head jerked in that direction as their hands dropped gun-wards.

Costain was first to recover, swinging back towards Reilly and jerking up his pistol.

But Reilly's saddle was empty and Costain never found out why because there was the sudden crack of a Colt from under the neck of the pony and Costain dropped, shot in the throat.

Without waiting for any further response, Reilly dived across the ten feet of space between him and the substantial water trough, landing short of his intended cover to roll through the dust, triggering his Colt as he did so.

Reilly's first shot caught Pablo in the chest, throwing the Mexican backwards, dead before he hit the ground. The cowboy's second drove into Kronos's shoulder, dropping him to the floor, badly wounded. Two of the remaining white men appeared to be trying to go two ways at once as, caught in the body by Reilly's remaining bullets, they too slumped floor-wards as Reilly twisted out of sight behind the sun-dried timber.

Parson, the only remaining Diablo so far unhurt,

hugged the planks of the veranda before lunging to his feet and driving towards Reilly's pony, emptying his pistol towards the water trough as he ran.

Like an avenging phantom, Reilly rose from behind the warped planks and his left-hand Colt spoke once. Caught in the head, Parson pitched forwards, yards from the dubious safety of the skittish pony.

Reilly was allowed no time to congratulate himself on his good shooting, because suddenly a voice was calling from behind the house.

'Fargo,' Dusty Rhodes was bellowing, 'that li'l bastard Rafe's got Miz Millie!'

No sooner were the words out of Rhodes's mouth than Rafe Carter appeared in the doorway of the shack, an arm across Millie Grafton's throat as he held the girl in front of him for a shield. Carter had barely reached the edge of the porch when a large calibre bullet smashed into the side of the water trough, splintering the sun-dried old wood and sending a gout of water skyward.

'I got plenty more where that one come from,' Karl Straker's voice quavered, still recognizable despite the distance. 'Put Rafe and Billy on their ponies and let 'em go, or I'm sure gonna plug somebody.'

Turning in the general direction of the voice, Reilly bellowed, 'Kronos can't ride and Miz Millie ain't going nowhere.'

'You're dead right, Miz Millie ain't goin' nowhere!' the girl agreed vehemently, struggling against her captor.

'You quit that, damn you,' Carter snarled, cocking his pistol and placing it next to the girl's forehead, provoking instant stillness. 'Get them horses,' Carter snarled, voice rising in uncontrolled hysteria. 'Get 'em or I'll let her have it here and now.'

For a moment, the girl's life hung in the balance, then Reilly's shoulders slumped.

'We're licked, get the horses, Dusty,' he intoned listlessly, raising his battered Stetson as he did so and scratching his head.

Up on the rim of the little basin, Long Travis caught the signal, snapped down the safety of his long-barrelled Winchester and moved back to collect his pony.

Why in hell Fargo hadn't just shot that little turd Rafe, he didn't know, but the past few days had taught the tall cowhand to respect his new-found friend's judgement. If Fargo said follow them, Long Travis was prepared to stay on their trail until hell froze, employing all the patience his Comanche upbringing had taught him.

Down by the cabin, Carter had managed to clamber on to a horse, with Millie seated in front of him. Next to him, Kronos sat slumped on the quietest pony in the remuda, cursing monotonously. Through the hole in his shirt, the wound in his shoulder showed red and inflamed.

'Nobody follows,' Carter whined, lifting his Colt meaningly, 'or you'll be collecting what's left of her in a box.'

'I oughta kill you, Reilly,' Kronos snarled, clinging desperately to his saddle, 'and one day I'm gonna. . . .'

'I'll be waitin',' Reilly interrupted. 'You can count on it.'

Abruptly, Reilly leapt back as the little group swept away in a swirl of dust.

'What happened, Dusty?' Reilly asked mildly, as the little horse breaker left the corner of the building where he had remained during the exchange.

'Bad luck,' Rhodes shrugged, 'or Billy was smarter than we thought. I'd bust out the window and got Miz Connie through when Rafe come in and grabbed Miz Millie.

'I wasted a cartridge on him but he was movin' too fast and time I was set again, well, he'd got Miz Millie and was dragging her outa the door.

'Ol' Rafe must be stronger than he looks,' Rhodes chuckled, ' 'cause Miz Millie was doin' her best to take his eye out. Would've managed it, too, if'n he hadn't half choked her. Girl's got sand, I'm tellin' you,' the old horse breaker finished.

'That's good,' Reilly said, ' 'cause she may need it afore we're finished. Saddle up, Dusty,' Reilly added, as Defoe puffed up, having quitted his position on the rim where he had been covering the group. 'We got business down trail.'

'What I don't understand,' Rhodes began, as he swung into the saddle, 'is why you didn't just let Long plug that li'l bastard Rafe soon as he got a good chance?'

'No good,' Reilly demurred. 'We need at least one of them, Rafe or Billy alive, or we got nothin' on Carter. So here's what I figger to do. . . .'

CHAPTER SIXTEEN

'Has anyone ever told you you're nuts, Fargo?' Bud Defoe asked with forced politeness

'Not for at least ten minutes,' Reilly answered, with a grin at his exasperated friend.

'It ain't that I'm not fond of a gamble, you'll understand,' Dusty Rhodes began from Reilly's other side, 'but if'n you're figgerin' on suicide, why d'you got to include us?'

The three men lay just below a ridge of rock, over-looking the night camp of Rafe Carter and his party.

Karl Straker had joined the group soon after leaving the Diablos' camp and, at first, they had made good time. Almost as good as Long Travis, who was patiently following them as well as leaving a clear trail for his friends.

Soon, however, the boiling sun had begun to dry out Kronos's wound, causing him to slow his mount to a walk, and with Millie compounding the awkward-ness of riding double in every way her fertile mind could devise, the final straw came when the pony Carter and the girl were riding pulled up dead lame.

'What in hell do we do now?' Straker whined, looking across at a half-delirious Billy Kronos.

'Fort up,' Carter decided, looking round anxiously. Gradually, his bloated face cleared after examining the entrance to the rocky gap where they had been forced to stop.

'We're in luck, Karl boy,' he enthused. 'We can set up camp over there,' he began, pointing to the back of the rocky valley, some four hundred yards away. 'They can't shoot down on us without hittin' the girl,' he went on, 'an' we only gotta watch the front. It's perfect.'

Now, as darkness fell, Reilly saw Carter put a single end of wood on the tiny fire of mesquite before settling down with his rifle over his knees, watching the gap in the rock which marked the entrance to their camp ground. Behind him, in an angle of the rocky wall and as far from the group as she could get, the girl squirmed down into her blankets.

'See,' Reilly began, with an enthusiasm he was far from feeling, 'Miz Millie's back out of the firelight and them boys are too lazy to collect enough wood for a big fire. All I gotta do is throw a rope down that chimney near where she's layin', shinny down it and—'

'Get yourself killed,' Defoe interrupted, with a discontented growl.

'Why don't I just plug Rafe from here?' Long Travis demanded. 'It'd sure save a lot of trouble and would be my especial pleasure.'

'I told you,' Reilly answered patiently, 'I need li'l Rafe alive, Billy and Straker too, if'n I can manage it.'

'May as well get on with it,' Reilly went on, with one last look at the peaceful camp ground. 'Don't forget, now. Keep Miz Connie safe and when you start shootin' . . . make sure you miss.'

It was the snapping crack of a Winchester that brought Rafe Carter out of his uneasy doze. Without thinking, sure that the camp must be under attack, he leapt up, discarding his rifle and darting towards the prone form of the girl, still unaccountably huddled beneath her blankets.

As he reached down to grasp the girl's wrist, he noticed Straker throwing back his blankets and reaching for his rifle.

'Karl,' Carter bellowed, 'watch the gap! I've got the girl!'

Pulling hard, Carter made to drag the girl to her feet. She came easily, too easily for Carter's comfort as, caught off balance he staggered backwards, only to receive a rock-like fist to the point of the chin as he turned back towards her.

Badly shaken and only half conscious, he staggered backwards as Straker, ten yards behind him, screamed, 'Christ, Rafe, it's Reilly!' before slamming his rifle to his shoulder and triggering a wild shot.

Reilly cursed, shaking himself free of the encumbering blankets he had occupied after silently spiriting Millie away, as, caught in the spine by the Sharps' enormous bullet, Rafe Carter was thrown forward, jerking once, then to lie ominously still.

Without a glance at Straker's victim, Reilly lunged forward as Straker, seeing his danger, dropped his treasured Sharps and jerked at his pistol.

Straker's weapon came clear of his holster, just as Reilly's iron fingers closed on the man's wrist. For a brief moment, the pair struggled until a shot rang out and one of the figures slumped and dropped away.

'Fargo, for Christ's sake,' Bud Defoe was calling as he raced towards the single figure, palming a battered Colt as he ran. 'Are you all right?'

The figure on its feet raised a hand, palm outwards, in the universal Indian sign for peace, as it said in Fargo Reilly's voice. 'Stop your squawkin', Bud, I ain't killed just yet.' Disgust was heavy in his tones as he went on, 'But I sure managed to make a hash o' this, though.'

Rafe Carter was dead. Straker's heavy slug had shattered the Circle C man's spine and he had probably lived bare seconds after falling to the ground. Straker was dead too, or at least as good as, with a belly wound that no amount of attention from Connie and Millie could keep from bleeding.

Disgustedly, Reilly turned away, walking out of the circle of firelight to where Long Travis was examining the prone form of Billy Kronos with the aid of a makeshift torch.

'You did better than you thought,' Travis began callously. 'Bullet chipped a piece outa his lung, looks like.' The tall cowboy shrugged. 'Slug's still in there and he's bleedin' inside,' he paused as Kronos coughed breathily, the red stain apparent on his lips even in the poor light of the torch.

'Blood poisoning 'll finish him if the slug don't. I'm guessin' he won't last 'til mornin'.'

'And you're sure a good guesser,' came in a croak from the wounded man. The effort to speak was almost too much, but Kronos managed a weak laugh as Reilly knelt by his side, the badge on his shirt catching the torch light.

'Looks like you lose, deppity,' the Circle C foreman sneered weakly. 'With me and the rest dead, no one can testify against Lucas and you ain't got one single . . . smid . . . gen . . . o' . . .eviden . . . ce, God damn your soul to hell. Lucas can stand . . . pat an' . . . you can't. . . .'

Kronos lapsed into mumbling incoherence, and Reilly came lithely to his feet, his agile mind examining a desperate plan, the seeds of which had been planted by Kronos's last words.

'Fargo,' Defoe called from the fire. 'Straker just died.'

'Bud, is there a land office or an agent in Verdad? Someone who can record a land deed?' Reilly demanded brusquely, apparently ignoring his friend's words.

'Sure,' Defoe confirmed wonderingly, as he flicked the blanket over Straker's staring eyes. 'Phil Gainor, who used to be the manager of the bank afore Wilson was brought in, handles all that business. He must be kinda hard pushed,' Defoe went on conversationally, 'so he took over the day to day stuff at the bank, when Wilson got shot. Though I'm guessin',' the old peace officer finished shrewdly, 'Carter don't tell him no more than he needs to.'

'What sorta fella is this Gainor?' Reilly demanded.

'Good man for our sort o' town,' Defoe admitted,

142

wondering where this was going. 'Knows when and who to take a chance on and when to back away. Shrewd, too,' he added.

'Hmm, sounds like just the sorta man I had in mind. You ever play poker with Carter, Long?' Reilly demanded inconsequentially, as the tall one approached the fire, leading one of the ponies.

'Sure,' Travis admitted. 'Took money off'n him a coupla times.'

'Good player?' Reilly asked.

'He would be,' Travis admitted judiciously, ' 'cept he likes to gamble too much.'

'Sort to discard three of a kind 'cause he can only see the straight that he could make, if that's any help,' Rhodes added.

'Not the sort to stand pat on what he's got, then?' Reilly asked, 'if he could gamble and get somethin' better?'

'About right,' Travis said patiently. Then unable to resist, he asked, 'You figgerin' on playin' him at poker sometime soon?'

'Mebbe not poker,' came the equable answer, 'but I've sure got another sort of a game I aim to run on him and . . . you boys are gonna help me.'

'I ain't sure I like the sound of this,' Travis remarked. 'We shoulda stuck to somethin' safe,' he finished, 'like stealin' horses.'

'Listen,' Reilly began, hunkering down by the dying embers of the camp fire and ignoring the tall one, 'this is how we're gonna play it. . . .'

'I said it afore and I'm sure aimin' to say it again,'

Defoe snapped. 'If'n you ain't crazy, you're the near-est thing to it I ever seen wearin' pants.'

'What d'you think, Dusty?' Reilly demanded, ignoring the apoplectic peace officer.

'It all depends on whether you're readin' Carter right,' Rhodes began shrewdly. 'And if this here Gainor'll play?' he finished, turning to the marshal with a lifted eyebrow.

'Phil'll be OK,' Defoe responded confidently. 'He ain't got no more use for Carter and his methods than we have.'

'Well, that settles it,' Rhodes offered. 'After all, Fargo, it's your neck you're gamblin' with.'

'Sure, and if'n I don't,' Reilly stated, 'them kids and their ma lose everything. Let's ride,' he ordered. 'Me and Bud gotta be in Verdad before first light, day after tomorrow.'

'Huh?' Travis responded inelegantly.

'That day, at noon,' Defoe snapped, before Reilly could respond, 'Black Mesa gets sold at auction.'

It was, in fact, some hours before dawn when Reilly and Defoe pulled their exhausted ponies to a halt in the shelter of the battered lean-to which served the jail as a stable.

Seemingly impervious to the fatigues of almost twenty-four hours spent continually in the saddle, Reilly slipped from his mount and handed the reins to a weary Bud Defoe.

'Wake Gainor up and square him,' Reilly ordered. 'I got some business to attend to.'

*

Despite the lateness of the hour, business in the Long Branch was still brisk, Lucas Carter noted with satisfaction as he stooped to collect some of the night's takings from the box behind the bar.

Leaving sufficient cash in the box for his still busy bar staff to make change, Carter turned to the stairs leading to his office, apparently ignoring the two gun-hung hard cases who fell in behind him.

Reaching his opulent second-floor office, Carter paused under the single oil-lamp that had been left burning by his door as one of his duo of guards drew a pistol and pushed through the heavy oak door and into the office.

A moment later the man was out.

'OK, Boss,' the man said.

'Good, now get back to the bar-room,' Carter snapped. 'I ain't payin' you to stand around here.'

Waiting until the men had descended the stairs, Carter let himself into the office, locked the door behind him and deposited the sack of bills and notes on his desk, smiling fatly at their solid weight.

About to pour himself a drink, Carter paused, grimacing irritably, as there came a knocking on the study door. Without a word, the fat man snapped back the lock and jerked the door open.

'What in hell . . .' Carter began, then he stopped because he found himself looking into the bore of a rock-steady Colt below a pair of icy blue eyes, both features being the property of Mr Fargo Reilly.

CHAPTER SEVENTEEN

A single flick of the Colt's barrel sent Carter backing into the opulent study and then the fat man was watching in amazement as the weapon twirled casually on Reilly's finger to nestle back in its holster, apparently of its own volition.

'I think it's time you and me had a little talk, Mr Carter,' Reilly began mildly. 'We need to clear up a few misunderstandings and . . . eh . . . d'you mind if I call you Lucas?'

'So what's in this deal for you?' Carter demanded after Reilly had finished his explanation. 'Federal marshal and all, why should I trust you?'

'Money,' Reilly answered simply. 'I persuade Sanchez to sell at your price, say one hundred and fifty thousand dollars and for that I get, oh, say . . . five per cent of what we make . . . partner. Which then allows me to . . . eh . . . retire to a life of well earned luxury.

'A hundred and fifty thousand . . . where in hell do I get that kinda money?' Carter demanded.

'Don't be stupid, Lucas,' Reilly returned silkily. 'That's less than a dollar an acre and once you've got water on the place, which with that federal grant old man Sanchez figgered out ain't gonna cost you a penny, it'll be worth at least ten times that. Mebbe a hundred times . . . or more.'

'You run the bank,' Reilly finished. 'Ain't you got any idea how you might raise that sorta cash?'

For a long second Carter stared into space and Reilly wondered if the fat man had seen through what might have seemed, to any sane man at least, a wholly implausible scheme.

Only greed might be the deciding factor, since Reilly knew quite well that his price was some hundred thousand dollars below what Carter had been willing to pay Raoul Sanchez. That, and a desire to see Luis Sanchez crawling off his father's ranch.

'I'll go with you,' Carter suddenly snapped, jerking out of his reverie, 'but for that five per cent, you gotta get Wilson's letter.'

'Can't be did,' Reilly answered, shaking his head, 'but don't worry. Defoe won't make no trouble if'n you don't try and run that mortgage scam on young Sanchez.'

'Come to think of it,' he went on,' if you play it right you could make that letter work for you. Listen, when you start the auction. . . .'

Noon of that day found the bar-room of the Long Branch packed to its not inconsiderable capacity.

Almost the whole town had come to see a man's life's work bartered away under the auctioneer's hammer.

'You're sure this is gonna work, Dusty?' Luis Sanchez demanded for only about the twentieth time since the idea had been explained to him.

'Nothin's sure in life, boy,' Travis growled from his place at the bar next to Sanchez, before his old-time friend and partner could answer. 'But if Fargo says so, this is sure your best shot. Besides,' the tall one added matter-of-factly, 'Carter holds all the aces. You ain't got no choice.'

'*Sí, Patron,*' Diego Morales, now Sanchez's *segundo*, urged.' You're gonna lose Black Mesa either way. At least like this, you gotta chance.'

'Get set,' Dusty Rhodes snapped, as Carter and Lane Walker, accompanied by an uncharacteristically smug looking Fargo Reilly, emerged from the fat man's second-floor office and made their way down the saloon's broad staircase.

'Long . . .' Rhodes began, then he stopped because he was talking to himself. Long Travis was already forcing his way through the crowd to the main door of the saloon, his heavy calibre Winchester cradled easily in the crook of one arm, keen old eyes scanning the doorways on the second-floor balcony.

Reaching the floor of the saloon Reilly paused, pushing back his Stetson with a middle finger before carelessly scratching his left ear. From his place next to Sanchez, Dusty Rhodes moved a finger to his beaky nose and began to edge sideways through the crowd, apparently ignoring Bud Defoe, who was standing idly at the other end of the bar, sawn-off balanced easily in the crook of his right arm.

A low chair and table had been placed in front of the bar and with much puffing and wheezing, Carter managed to lever himself on to the latter to stand breathing heavily as he surveyed the crowd.

'Friends,' he began pompously. 'You're all here today to see young Luis Sanchez there,' he paused, pointing at the clearly uncomfortable young man, 'have his ranch auctioned to pay his pa's mortgage. But I have discovered that there has been foul dealin', friends.' He paused, waiting for the shocked muttering to die down.

'Because of this,' Carter went on, 'I'm tearin' up his pa's mortgage and I'm offerin' to buy Black Mesa from him for one hundred and fifty thousand dollars!'

'Marshal Defoe here,' Carter went on, when the noise had subsided, 'is gonna check this document.'

The mortgage was handed to Bud Defoe, who examined it minutely, before handing it to Luis Sanchez who scanned it before finally nodding his head.

'Well, go ahead boy, you tear it up,' Carter beamed expansively. 'And what about my offer?'

Without hesitation, Sanchez tore the document to shreds before looking up and saying, 'That land'd be worth a hell of a lot more with water on it!'

'But you ain't gonna get water on it,' Reilly interrupted impatiently. 'You can't fight Carter and his dollars, boy!' he insisted vehemently. 'Better you sell.'

149

Momentarily, Sanchez seemed about to argue, then his shoulders slumped.

'Where do I sign?' he mumbled disconsolately.

'That's the spirit:' Carter agreed. 'Just come in the office and you, Gainor,' he snapped at a cold-eyed, grey-haired man in a neat broadcloth suit, 'bring them papers.'

Ten minutes later, Luis Sanchez emerged from the second-floor office, followed by an expansive Lucas Carter.

'Drinks all round, boys,' Carter boomed. 'I want all you men to help me celebrate! I've just become the biggest man in these parts.'

'You may want to hold off on that celebration, Carter,' Reilly offered mildly, his cold tone cutting through the general conversation and stopping it as though he had turned off a tap.

Careful not to take his eyes from Lane Walker, Reilly edged up to the bar and held out several crumpled, dog-eared pieces of paper, which he had previously eased carefully from an inside pocket.

'You may want to read this,' he began, eyes never leaving the little gunman, while Long Travis by the front door clicked down the safety of his Winchester and gave all his attention to a slowly opening door on the second-floor balcony.

'What in hell is this?' Carter began, face twisting angrily.

'Read it,' Reilly said simply.

Reilly watched as the fat man began to read, the disbelief growing on the jowly face.

'For the rest of us,' Reilly went on, apparently ignoring Walker as the little gunman began to edge away from the bar, 'I can tell you that what Mr Carter is holdin' in his hand is a report by a federal engineer which says, once you get past the high-falutin' talk, that there ain't no way to irrigate Black Mesa. Ground's all wrong and any dam you threw across the river'd just break up and float downstream.

'The bank's just rotten,' Reilly finished, 'and Black Mesa ain't never gonna be nothin' but sheep pasture.'

'B-b-but I just paid that goddam greaser a hundred and fifty thousand. . . . Dammit I want my goddam money back.'

'Deed's recorded,' Phil Gainor said with slow relish. 'Recorded and there ain't nothin' you can do about it,' he finished, easing backwards to stand behind Bud Defoe and his ever-ready shotgun.

'Looks like you lose, Carter,' Reilly said easily. 'Seems to me,' he went on judiciously, 'about your only way out is to sell your holdin's, try and square the bank. Now I wonder,' he went on slowly, 'where we might find an *hombre* who'd take the Circle C and Black Mesa off'n your hands for . . . oh . . . say . . . about a hundred and fifty thousand dollars?'

For a moment, it looked as if Carter might give in quietly.

Then gradually his face began to mottle, hands lifting to clench and unclench in the air above his head. Almost it seemed he found it impossible to speak, the pressure of his feelings making it impossible for them to find an outlet.

151

'You!' he spat suddenly, glaring at his tormentors. 'You! How long have you had that paper?'

'Found Corcoran about four days ago,' Reilly answered equably. 'Paper was in his pocket. Just got back in time to go after them Diablo skunks.'

'They're all dead, Carter, by the way,' Defoe threw in, 'all of them. Including Rafe.'

For a moment, Carter looked at the elderly peace officer as though he hadn't heard.

'That's right, Carter,' Defoe went on, with relish, 'Billy Kronos, Straker, Rafe and the others. All dead. But Rafe talked before he died and—'

But Carter was rallying from the shock now and he swept a hand over his face before snarling, 'That don't mean nothin'. Whatever that stupid little bastard might've said, none of it'll stand up in a court of law. And I'll get my own engineer in and submit my own report to the governor. Then—'

'That mebbe won't be as simple as you think,' Reilly interrupted. 'I wired a copy of Corcoran's report to the governor's office and the federal surveyor's department, who Corcoran worked for. I ain't had a reply yet but I guess they'll sure want one o' their own men to check anything you send to 'em.'

'Now.' Reilly went on reasonably, 'like I said, you better think about sellin' your land. I just might know someone who'd have that sort a money available.'

'Oh and don't forget my five per cent,' Reilly finished. 'I'm aimin' to turn it over to Miz Millie. I figger it should just cover the cost o' the damage your boys did to the *Tribune*'s office.'

For a long moment, Carter simply stood, the colour mounting from his bull-like neck, enpurpling his face until it almost seemed that he must erupt, like a long-forgotten volcano.

Suddenly, there was a spurt of crimson from his nose, which turned into a gushing torrent.

Desperately, Carter slapped a gaudy handkerchief to his face and when the last of the gore had been wiped away, he turned to Reilly.

His nose was still swollen but his face was somehow calm, as though the rush of blood had eased the pressure in his mind as well as his bloated body.

'I should've killed you.' Carter began, almost reflectively, 'you and that goddam trick horse. . . .'

'That's been your trouble all along, Lucas,' Reilly said softly. 'You left too many loose ends.'

'Fortunately,' Carter snarled, voice rising to a scream, 'that's one goddam thing that can be remedied! Get 'im, boys.'

And almost before the words were out of his boss's mouth, Lane Walkers' right hand was driving for his Colt, the weapon snapping clear of its holster and firing before anyone else could make a move.

CHAPTER EIGHTEEN

Well, before almost anybody could move, that is.

Walker's bullet tore Reilly's Stetson from his head but, as an echo of the little gunman's weapon, Reilly's Colt bellowed, driving his first shot into Walker's chest, followed by a second and third, all three bullets slicing in so close together that the holes would have needed only a single playing card to cover them.

Cocking the hammer of his battered Colt as it recoiled in his fist, Reilly jerked a card table off its legs, dropping behind its scant shelter and driving a bullet into the fleshy part of Carter's leg as the fat man scuttled behind the bar.

Without hesitation, Reilly fired his fifth shot into the front of the bar, before palming his second Colt and deliberately emptying its five rounds into the solid timber, ignoring Defoe and Dusty Rhodes, who had swiftly covered the remaining Circle C hands, and Long Travis who, with clinical precision, was in the process of fatally perforating Carter's two body-guards as they exited the second-floor room where they had been hidden, awaiting their boss's summons.

Sam Colt's brainchild, known variously as the Colt Peacemaker or Frontier model Colt is often referred to as a six-shooter. But every old-time Westerner who ever used one, loaded only five chambers leaving the sixth empty and under the hammer, so as not to shoot themselves in the foot if the pistol hammer happened to be jerked inadvertently.

Carter, of course, knew this, and although not a gunman by trade, he also knew enough to count his adversary's shots.

And so it was that he rose from behind the bar, face disfigured by an evil leer, as he brought up his still-loaded pistol to point in Reilly's direction.

'Fargo, look out,' Rhodes yelled, unable to spare his attention or his Colts' from their job of covering Carter's cowhands.

'He can't do nothin' . . .' Carter began, lining his pistol carefully.

Suddenly, a Colt cracked in the stillness and Carter was looking down unbelievingly at a red stain that disfigured his white shirt-front, spreading rapidly.

The fat man looked up to where Reilly stood, his pistol still smoking from the last shot that had smashed into Carters' chest.

'How . . .' the erstwhile owner of the Circle C began, then the whites of his eyes turned upwards as, pistol slipping from nerveless fingers, he slumped to the floor.

Keeping his second pistol trained on his victim,

Reilly eased the fat man over with the toe of his boot. Such precautions were plainly unnecessary, the welling red stain and glazed unseeing eyes told the whole story.

Unconcernedly, Reilly clicked open the loading gate of his Colt and began to reload the cylinder, as Long Travis. pausing only to confirm his good shooting, halted beside his friend and looked down at the late and unlamented owner of the Long Branch and Circle C ranch.

'I thought he'd got you, Fargo, I surely did. When you was fool enough to empty both pistols, I sure thought he'd got you,' Travis observed drily, clicking down his rifle safety and beginning to push cartridges into the magazine. 'How in hell d'you work it?'

'Afore I went to see him, I loaded up the empty chambers.' Reilly answered simply. 'I figgered he'd never think I'd got a couple extra and he weren't man enough to shoot it out, unless he figgered to have a real good edge. He'd have quit like the coyote he was, hired a fancy lawyer and that wouldn't've done nobody any good.'

'No,' Reilly went on, snapping shut the loading gate of his second Colt and slipping it into its worn, greasy holster. 'This way was best for everybody. Saved me a pile o' paper work and the state the expense of a trial. Only the lawyers lose out, which I figger means a happy ending all round.

'Look after things here, will you, Bud?' Reilly called across to the marshal, who was engaged in disarming the remains of the Circle C contingent.

'Me and Luis got to see Mr Gainor about a few things,' he explained as he took the young Mexican by the arm.

'Such as?' Defoe demanded, but with no real heat.

'Circle C and Black Mesa are now the bank's property and I figger Mr Gainor may be open to a reasonable offer for both places. Say . . . oh . . . about a hundred and fifty thousand US,' came the mild reply.

'It was Long or Dusty put me on to it first,' Reilly admitted, lounging at ease in Defoe's office and cradling a glass. Pecos stood patiently at the rail, saddle-bags packed.

It was a week after Carter's death and Reilly, who was leaving, had stopped by for a last drink with Defoe.

'I forget which,' he admitted, 'but one of 'em said, Carter had been a farmer in Missouri. O'course, one look at the soil on Black Mesa would've told any farmer what that sorta land was worth and that's why Carter was tryin' to get his hands on it.'

'We all figgered Raoul was tetched,' Defoe admitted, 'way he went on about Black Mesa bein' a paradise but Carter musta realized Raoul was right.'

'That's certain,' Reilly agreed. 'He'd got rid of all the other little men down along the river, using the Diablos, but Raoul Sanchez was being stubborn. Carter must've thought it was his lucky day when Sanchez offered to sell. Then Raoul was killed and Carter figgered to save hisself some money by gettin' Wilson to forge that title. What he had on Wilson, I guess we won't never know, but there musta bin somethin'.'

'Guess it don't matter much now,' Defoe said meditatively, 'so I burned the letter without opening it,' he added, before Reilly asked his question.

'Best thing all round,' Reilly admitted. 'Although,' he added thoughtfully, 'Carter's luck was real good to find hisself with a bank manager who he could blackmail so convenient. And I sure wonder how he found out whatever it was he had on Wilson.'

'They're both dead, so I guess it don't matter much,' Defoe reiterated. 'But what I still don't get,' he admitted, 'is how Corcoran was killed?'

'Raoul Sanchez did it,' Reilly shrugged. 'That's why he was about to take a shot at me when Straker shot him, actin' on Kronos's orders, I'm guessin, 'cause it was sure a cinch Carter didn't want him killed.

'I'm figgerin' Corcoran, who the federal marshal's office have had their eye on for a while,' Reilly went on, 'tried to blackmail the old man. They fought and Corcoran was killed. I found a stone with blood and a little hair on it in the cave with Corcoran's body, so that's sure how it looked to me. Might even have been an accident.'

'So then knowing, after all these years, that Black Mesa was worthless, he set Carter up. What d'you figger Raoul was gonna do when Carter found out the ranch was no good?' Defoe asked.

'Mebbe he never thought that far,' Reilly shrugged, standing up and settling his hat. 'From what I've heard, he wasn't a real deep planner. Guess that's somethin' else we'll never know.'

Silently, the two shook hands and Defoe accompanied his friend to the hitch rail, standing by as he swung into the saddle.

'I'll see you, Bud,' was Reilly's only farewell and then he was gone, riding alone into the strong south-western sunlight.

'I sure hope not,' Defoe murmured as he turned away.